Contents

Prologue vii

A New Beginning 1
The Master's Voice 7
Reflection and Direction 16
The Search 22
Open Doors 27
Defying Darkness 35
Not Yet 45
Continuing On 51
Here to Help 55
The Jamisons 64
Perfect! 75
Strange Happenings 83
Right Prevails 92
Time for Celebration 100
Sinister Plots Revealed 104
Peace Fields 109
Preparation 118
Dedication 124
Chart the Course 131
Little Boy Lost 138

Epilogue 149
About the Author 151

With Faith and Love
Continue the Journey
Love,
Sue

WHERE CEDARS *Sing*

ES HYDE

WestBow Press
A DIVISION OF THOMAS NELSON
& ZONDERVAN

Copyright © 2016 ES Hyde.

All rights reserved. No part of this book may be used or reproduced by any means, graphic, electronic, or mechanical, including photocopying, recording, taping or by any information storage retrieval system without the written permission of the author except in the case of brief quotations embodied in critical articles and reviews.

Scripture taken from the King James Version of the Bible.

This is a work of fiction. All of the characters, names, incidents, organizations, and dialogue in this novel are either the products of the author's imagination or are used fictitiously.

WestBow Press books may be ordered through booksellers or by contacting:

WestBow Press
A Division of Thomas Nelson & Zondervan
1663 Liberty Drive
Bloomington, IN 47403
www.westbowpress.com
1 (866) 928-1240

Because of the dynamic nature of the Internet, any web addresses or links contained in this book may have changed since publication and may no longer be valid. The views expressed in this work are solely those of the author and do not necessarily reflect the views of the publisher, and the publisher hereby disclaims any responsibility for them.

Any people depicted in stock imagery provided by Thinkstock are models, and such images are being used for illustrative purposes only. Certain stock imagery © Thinkstock.

ISBN: 978-1-5127-4187-2 (sc)
ISBN: 978-1-5127-4189-6 (hc)
ISBN: 978-1-5127-4188-9 (e)

Library of Congress Control Number: 2016907571

Print information available on the last page.

WestBow Press rev. date: 5/17/2016

Prologue

Looking into the rearview mirror, Elizabeth saw the road behind her evaporate into nothingness. *Not so unlike my life*, she mused. Before her lay a strange new road—a road taking her—where? Instead of the fear that such a question might have brought, she felt incredible peace. The tightness that had been in her chest for months was gone now, as if mighty hands had released her very heart, soul, and spirit. What was to come she could not begin to imagine. Only God could bring beauty from ashes. Only He could use great pain in one life to alleviate suffering in another.

Elizabeth would learn to go beyond herself even into uncharted waters, allowing her to be an instrument of healing for others and in so doing begin her own journey toward wholeness. In a surreal moment, she could no longer see anything around her, only the rising sun before her. Being drawn toward the first light of day, she saw a little country church. She slowed and read their sign: "For we know that all things work together for good to them that love God, to those who are the called according to his purpose" (Romans 8:28).

Those words were going to play in her head over and over in the days to come as she dealt with unscrupulous characters and uncomfortable situations. She knew there would be loneliness ahead. As a child, the many days of loneliness and solitude had not bothered her. She had come to enjoy and actually embrace them. Always she knew there would be the sound of the familiar footsteps of her mama and brother coming down the path. She was safe. Now those footsteps would be no more. Would she ever be safe again?

Even as that question reverberated in her brain, another Scripture brought the answer. Elizabeth was very familiar with the truth of John 12:24: "Except a grain of wheat fall into the ground and die; it abideth alone: but if it die, it bringeth forth much fruit." She had tasted the death of many things and now "in God's timing" was ready to rise like the phoenix from the ashes.

There are so many people I need to thank for their help in making this book happen.

I must thank my son, Jimmy, for his patience and for the hours he put in trying to get everything just the way I wanted it. He even took the picture of my grandson, Jay, at Linville Falls, North Carolina, and turned it into the book cover.

To Donna Jill: Thank you, my dear prayer partner, for your encouragement. You believed in me when I was not sure I could go on.

To Leslie: Thank you, girlfriend. Only you and I know of the work you did. Without your help, this book would not have happened.

To my precious children and grandchildren, who are always there for me!

And to Wes LeRoy and the wonderful people of West-Bow Press: I am so grateful that God led me to them.

A New Beginning

It was almost dusk when Elizabeth Barrington entered the tiny town of Leesboro, Virginia. She had arrived in the Blue Ridge Mountains with a big, furry cat named Uggy, all her earthly belongings, and a heart full of hope for the future. Her place was on the other side of town about two miles out, so in Leesboro that meant she would be living in the country. Some of the locals respectfully tipped their hats as she slowly drove by. She could feel their small-town questions, but she just smiled back and continued on.

Elizabeth hadn't intended to be so late getting home. *Home!* Yes, Cedar Grove was now her home. On the trip up, she had shed tears of trepidation, but now as she started up the tree-lined drive, she smiled and again wiped away tears, but these were tears of joy at the peace she felt deep within. As a bird taking flight, the long days and nights of displacement and the weight of uncertainty had lifted. She had spent many hours in agonizing prayer, and God had given His answer. He had brought her here. She was as certain of that as she had ever been of anything.

Instead of stopping in front of the rambling old farmhouse, she made her way down the tiny, winding drive to the cabin in back. She would at least let Doc know she had arrived. But it wasn't Doc who came bounding out to greet her.

"Hello, Joe Bob! So good to see you!" she said as the young man jerked the truck door open with such force she wondered what kept it on the hinges.

"Hey, Ms. Liz-beth. I been waiting for ya all day long, and now you're here!"

Just then, Doc and Anna Louise came down the steps to greet her. This little family of two brothers and a sister was a wonderful living testimony to God's love in human hearts. She was so grateful that they had been placed in her life. She didn't know all of what God was doing, of course, but she knew He was caring for her the way a shepherd tends to an injured lamb, and she felt safe, warm, and secure. Those were feelings she had longed for all her life, and now she was going to try to live in such a way as to show her gratitude to Him for it.

Doc's gentle voice pulled her back to reality as he told her that the heat was on at her house and that Anna Louise had left a fresh cake of corn bread on the table. She thanked them and assured them that she didn't want to unload the truck until morning. The trip had been tiring, and she just wanted a long, hot bath and a good night's sleep. She was here to stay this time, so there was no hurry.

Waving good-bye, she carefully turned the truck around and made her way up the long, narrow drive to her own back door. Darkness was beginning to settle in, with only thin fingers of sunlight piercing through the thick evergreens. She was very glad that the newly installed motion sensor lights were operating correctly. The shadows were eerie and caused Elizabeth to move quickly up the back steps. This big old house had become hers only a few months before, but it already felt familiar. She knew exactly how to maneuver the heavy, ancient key in the lock and how high to reach to grasp the string that would turn on the single light bulb and illuminate the room. Now bathed in inviting light, she let her eyes drink in everything about the big, comfortable country kitchen.

She especially loved the worn, paint-chipped Hoosier cabinet with its pullout counter and special flour bin with the hand-crank sifter. And that huge old range with the four units, the center warming area, and its built-in deep well. She had never seen anything like that before. It had a huge turkey-baking size oven and a smaller one too. Under these was a drawer large enough to hold every baking pan she would ever need.

Probably her favorite piece, though, was the 1940s "Frigadairy," as she had heard many of the locals refer to the refrigerator. It had a tiny little freezer compartment that held two metal ice trays, and it ran so quietly that she often pulled on the big wooden handle just to peek inside, fearing it had died. She loved the wee bulb ... about the size of a Christmas tree light. It always seemed to smile and say, "Don't worry about us! We're still on the job!"

She really hoped she would have no need to replace any of these time-tested pieces. She could always put one of those big commercial freezers and modern monstrosity refrigerators out in the can house. It would be a bit inconvenient, but she would rather do that than spoil the charm of her vintage kitchen. She must take the time to send some really good pictures of this wonderful kitchen to her friend Bob, who was in the antique business back home. She knew Bob or his dad could tell her much about all these great pieces. It did not matter to her whether they were of any great monetary value or historical significance, but it would be fun to know something more about them. Perhaps that would give her even more insight about the people who used them in this particular home. Oh, there was much more work to do, and she wanted to oversee even the most minute, mundane detail. Now that she was going to be here full time, maybe the work would go a bit faster.

Uggy came out of the car carrier like a shot when Elizabeth opened its latch. She was glad she had brought it all the way inside before opening it. As heavy and cumbersome as it had been, it was still better than trying to round up a frightened cat in the dark and in strange surroundings. As she watched him cautiously moving around the room, she realized just how special he was to her. At times, he was a force to be reckoned with. He weighed well over twenty pounds and had long, bushy hair that made him look even bigger and quite formidable. She had seen him protect his turf from every other cat in the neighborhood. And his intimidating stance and low, hissing growl had kept most dogs—and people—at bay. Martin had never gotten along very well with him, and that brought a smile now too.

Her overnight bag and the basket of perishables must be brought in, but the rest could wait until morning. It wasn't really late, but after she fed Uggy and sat down with a glass of milk and a big piece of Anna Louise's delicious corn bread, she realized just how tired she was.

She had started out early that morning, but there had been so many tedious loose ends to deal with that she hadn't gotten on the road until after noon. Then she had driven even more carefully than usual. Although she had bought the truck several weeks before, it still felt strange to her. It was bigger than anything she had ever driven, and now with it loaded to the gills, it felt awfully heavy. She was painfully aware, too, that this vehicle would have to last her for a very long time, so she must treat it accordingly. She hoped there wouldn't be any need to haul more building materials, for two reasons. *Don't want to haul 'em in my new truck, and don't want to spend any more money on materials! Time to move on to something else!*

The house was toasty warm, and again Elizabeth silently breathed a prayer of thanksgiving. She went from the kitchen to her quarters and started her bath. She splurged by using some of the expensive lavender bath salts, even added some bubble bath, and settled into the steaming water. Just one more thing she loved about her old house: the big, deep, claw-foot bathtub. One could completely submerge in those things! The combination of warmth, pleasant aroma, and inner peace almost put her to sleep. She lingered until the water began to cool, and even then she reluctantly stepped out and wrapped herself in a soft, velvety bath sheet. She tiptoed quickly over the cold wood floor into her bedroom. Like everything else in this wonderful house, the room was oversized, and she loved it.

Her grandmother's old featherbed with its towering high-posters were drawing her in for a restful night's sleep. As she slipped between the crisp, white sheets, she allowed her eyes to drink in every captivating detail of the room. She had positioned her bed so she could look directly into the cavernous opening of the rock fireplace. How many times had she wished for a fireplace in her bedroom? She had broached the subject with Martin years ago when they were talking *again* about building their dream house. He had quickly dismissed it, saying how foolish something like that would be—just too messy and too expensive to use and keep up.

On that first day, she had marveled at the beautifully carved figures on the wormy chestnut mantle, both this one and the one just behind it in the parlor. Someone had been very artistic and had spent long hours creating, obviously with love, fine pieces of art. In both rooms she had hung antique mirrors on the hooks over the mantles, hooks that must have at one time held a heavy firearm. This house was well over one hundred years old, and such firearms were essential to any family of that era. A gun could have kept the family safe from intruders or perhaps it brought down a sixteen-point buck or a growling black bear. Hunting and bringing home wild meat was a common practice and necessary to take these early families through long, hard winters. She smiled as she allowed her imagination to see the man of the house carrying home still-warm wild turkeys for Thanksgiving and Christmas dinners.

Smiling, she let her eyes travel to the little room to the left of the fireplace that she had quickly turned into her walk-in closet. She would have no real need now for the many pairs of shoes she has once found so necessary or the after-five dresses and formal wear. She couldn't see herself using them here. Strange how good she felt about that. But she did like being able to have her clothes ironed and well organized, whether they were jeans and T shirts or housedresses and aprons. This little room probably was not built for that purpose at all. She felt sure it has been the nursery or "weaning room" for the many babies who had entered the world in this very bedroom. How safe they must have felt as they grew, moving from Mama's bed and arms to their own special bed just a few feet away.

She wanted to continue to study every nail and board in her room, for she knew they held stories that could enlighten and entertain her for eternity if she would only care for them respectfully and listen to them intently. But this momentous day was settling in on her tired body. Her eyelids were becoming extremely heavy as she felt Uggy pounce onto the bed and curl up at her feet. She could feel herself being transported to a land of contentment and peaceful dreams. She began her evening prayers but settled into a deep, restorative sleep before they were finished.

The Master's Voice

Elizabeth awakened to Uggy jumping from the bed and to sunlight streaming into the room through a gap in the curtain. *What time is it, what day ... and where am I anyway?* she thought. She felt all warm inside as reality came flooding over her. She pulled the quilt up close to her chin and scanned the room through sleepy eyes.

"Where am I?" she said aloud. "I'm home—that's where I am. I'm safe and secure in my home here at Cedar Grove, where God brought me!" She chuckled to herself. "I hope no one is working outside yet. They'll hear me and decide that I really am that crazy old woman from the Smokies in there talking to herself."

Pulling on a heavy robe, Elizabeth made her way into the kitchen to put on coffee. She fed Uggy, but instead of letting him out, she decided he could just swallow his pride and *go* in the box until she was ready to go out with him. She knew he would want to explore this new place, but she wanted to keep an eye on him at his first outing.

It was still early, not yet seven, and there was such quiet around her that she decided the whole world must still be sleeping. As was her preferred way at morning time, she poured her delicate china cup of coffee, picked up her Bible, and climbed back into bed. She had forgotten to turn up the heat, but she was so snug and warm she would do that later. She knew she wouldn't get to enjoy her mornings this way much longer, but she would certainly do so while she could.

Sipping her coffee, she entered into a time of morning prayer. She had so much to be thankful for that the simplest reflection brought tears. She set her coffee cup down, and there in the still and quiet of the morning, she bowed her head and let her heart overflow. The tears flowed as waters that thunder over mountain falls. They were cleansing, calming, and soothing tears—tears that were washing away the debris that would hinder her communion with her Lord. When she lifted her head, dried her tears, and reached for her Bible, she knew her heart would now be able to "rightly divide the Word of truth" and receive guidance and strength and mercy and grace for the day that lay before her.

How very like God, she thought as she laid her Bible open to her devotional passage for the day. She began to read Psalm 101.

I will sing of mercy and judgment: unto thee, O Lord will I sing. I will behave myself wisely in a perfect way. O when wilt thou come unto me? I will walk within my house with a perfect heart. I will set no wicked thing before mine eyes: I hate the work of them that turn aside; it shall not cleave to me. A forward heart shall depart from me: I will not know a wicked person. Whoso privily slandereth his neighbor, him will I cut off: him that hath an high look and a proud heart will not I suffer. Mine eyes shall be upon the faithful of the land, that they may dwell with me: he that walketh in a perfect way, he shall serve me. He that worketh deceit shall not dwell within my house: he that telleth lies shall not tarry in my sight. I will early destroy all the wicked of the land: that I may cut off all wicked doers from the city of the Lord.

As she read through that passage and several more, she said aloud, "Amen and amen!" She would dedicate her new home from day one to God, and with His help and guidance, she would see that no *one* or no*thing* defiled it. Reflecting on past days, she knew that it wouldn't just happen, not without conscious effort on her part. But she also knew that with God's help, it could and would be possible, "for God *is,* and He is a rewarder of them that diligently seek him" (Hebrews 11:6).

After a time of refreshing worship, Elizabeth laid her Bible aside and went in to refill her cup. She turned up the heat and walked on through to the front of the house. A gentle rain had begun to fall, causing even the barren trees to take on such a bright, glistening beauty that she just stood and stared in wonder. Was this the most beautiful place on the planet, or was she just now looking through eyes that were learning to appreciate the beauty that was everywhere?

She had been there only a moment when the entire scene began to change before her very eyes. The rain was giving way to snow—beautiful, softly falling snow, drifting toward earth like the downy feathers of some giant heavenly fowl. There was no person alive who loved snow more than she. To Elizabeth, this was God's way of saying, "Welcome to your new abode, my child. Enjoy all that I have for you here. I created it for you, but the beauty you see before you now can in no way compare to the beauty of heaven that you will one day be allowed to enter into and enjoy for eternity!"

The heavy oak door groaned and creaked as she eased it open so she could step out onto the porch for a closer look. The cold air hit her like a thousand icy needles, causing her to gasp, and then she was reminded of the heavily laden truck. She must get it unloaded quickly. After all, this weather could easily turn mean in a hurry. There were things that must come on inside, but after that, being snowed in suited her just fine.

It was early February, still very much winter in these parts and an ideal time for mountain winter weather. Even in the Smokies, she had many times been forced to change Valentine's Day plans because of a snowstorm coming up quickly, covering the landscape with the most beautiful downy white comforter of snow. Elizabeth had allowed herself only until Easter to have everything at Cedar Grove ready for an "open house." That time was not set in stone, of course, but in her mind she was planning to have friends in for a dedication on Good Friday and then officially opening the following Friday. Since Easter came late this year, she felt that she was pretty much on track, but there could be no idle days if it were to all come together. With that thought, she quickly dressed and started out back to begin the task.

"Mornin', Ms. Elizabeth," called Anna Louise as she started toward the truck. She looked up to see the young woman hurrying up the drive with Joe Bob fast on her heels. It was such a comforting feeling to know that they were always there, just a whisper away.

"Good morning," she answered back. "What are you two doing out so early on this raw morning?"

"We're here to help you, Ms. Liz-beth. You need us," Joe Bob quickly answered her as he ran up to her and engulfed her in his big man/boy arms. "I'm strong, and I'm going to help you take your special things in the house—and I'll be real careful, won't I, Sister?"

"Of course you will, sweetie," said Anna Louise as she smoothed his hair. "We both will."

Elizabeth could hardly hold back the tears as she felt the love flowing from brother to sister and back again. She would soon learn of the suffering that this little family had dealt with, and yet they were the lights that illuminated the entire community, the glue that held the whole town together. She was learning more about love, faith, and perseverance every time she talked to someone here. Sometimes she felt that all her past years had been lived in a cocoon, but maybe now she was going to burst out. Oh, she wouldn't be a beautiful, soaring butterfly, but maybe at least she could add something of beauty to the world as she landed on a single blade of grass.

Already Anna Louise had deciphered Elizabeth's labeling system and was instructing Joe Bob as to where to take each box. Elizabeth hadn't known why she had chosen to identify boxes with pictures as well as with words, but now she knew. Without explanation Joe Bob knew that the smiley faces were on the boxes that went in the parlor and the cats were for Ms. Elizabeth's room. The magnolias, the roses, and the violets were equally easy for him.

In no time at all, everything was inside with no damage or mess. Elizabeth wondered why the whole world couldn't have been filled with wonderful people like these. At the same time, the answer came. These precious people had faced some very great tragedies, and yet they had yielded all to the sovereignty of God. He had molded them and made them as the potter with the clay, and now they were vessels of honor that He was using mightily. Their service might seem of little value to some, but Elizabeth could see that it was great before God, and to her they were ministering angels. He had caused their paths to cross at a time when she so needed human hands and hearts to help and to heal her. *Thanks be to God for leading me to them.*

Elizabeth tried her best to get both of them to have tea and sit and rest for a while, but Anna Louise explained that they needed to get on back and start some "dinner" for Doc. He had left early to go help a neighbor with a sick cow, and he'd be tired and hungry when he got back. She thought Joe Bob acted as if he wanted to stay, but he smiled big, gave her a bear hug, and followed his sister out. She walked out with them and moved the truck to its little spot at the edge of the front drive. That way if she did need to go out, even in the snow, at least it would be already headed downhill!

Elizabeth watched as the pair went quickly down the back drive toward their own little house. Anna Louise was zipping her brother's jacket and straightening his cap much as a mother would for a four-year-old. Joe Bob was a big, strong, young man who would always be a little boy. Doc had told her when she talked with him months before that Joe Bob was the most precious gift that God had given his family, and she was quickly learning the truth of that statement. Neither Doc nor Anna Louise ever considered him a burden; instead he was a tremendous joy. That they were both devoted to him was easy to see.

Just as she started the truck, the snow began to fall again with the most beautiful, delicate, huge flakes. Watching them stick on the icy limbs caused Elizabeth to know that soon the mountains were going to look like a perfect picture postcard. She had always lived in the mountains, so she knew how quickly the snow could transform even the bleakest countryside. That transformation of beauty could also turn brutal and bring tragedy in a moment. She had great respect for the power of nature and knew she was no match for it. She was very happy that Doc had showed her the generator in the barn. Although she had no mechanical ability, she had finally learned from him what to do ... just in case.

Even though the wind was picking up and chilling her through and through, she walked slowly back to the porch. In another life she would have bundled up and romped and played in the snow until she was exhausted. But not today. Today she would not be a child but an adult—an *old* adult woman who was alone and must be careful not to fall or get sick. She knew that it was up to her, just her and her faith in God, to make this new life work. Today she would enjoy the snow from inside—being sensible and cautious. *That's boring, but it is okay*, she thought as she let herself in. *I can still look out and build snowmen and ride sleds and throw snowballs in my mind and with my memories!*

Behind her, Elizabeth heard something scratching furiously. Uggy! She hadn't even thought of him. He must have run outside while they had been carrying in boxes. She jerked the door open, and he went past her so fast he almost knocked her backward. No need to worry about his getting disoriented; he knew exactly where he was and where he wanted to be—and it wasn't outside in this weather! He turned and looked at her so indignantly that she couldn't help laughing. She was glad that they had a special bond, for right now he was looking at her as if she were a mouse wearing catnip perfume! She found a towel, and he allowed her to dry him off, but he still gave her some strange looks and refused even the weakest purr. She poured him some fresh water and opened a can of his favorite Fancy Feast. He indignantly turned away. She knew he would withhold all affection as long as he chose but would end up on her bed when the day was done.

You big old lug, she thought. *What would I do without you?* He knew all her secrets, had seen all her tears, and had been there to love and be loved for a very long time. Good sense told her he would be gone someday—but she certainly wouldn't think of that until she had to.

As she prepared Uggy's food, she realized that she hadn't eaten anything yet today, and although it wasn't yet eleven o'clock, maybe she should go ahead and eat before she tackled the unpacking. She put a couple of eggs on to boil and prepared a big russet potato for baking. She was very glad she had bought an abundant supply of groceries at The Farmers Market as she came through Asheville. After all, she wasn't completely familiar with the markets in the area yet, so she thought it best to bring enough food to last for a while. She had not even given thought to being snowed in, but now as she looked out the window, that appeared to be a real possibility.

She fixed her food and poured a big glass of the Southern tea she had brought with her. Where she came from, that was tea so sweet others might have used it to sweeten their un-sweet. She used her beautiful crystal-stemmed goblet that had been her constant companion for as long as she could remember. She would enjoy her meal in the front parlor, where she could watch the falling snow. She reached for her newest Nicholas Sparks book but quickly laid it aside. She was being entertained by the bending and swaying of the trees in the strong wind. She was sure she could hear them howling, groaning, and moaning as they tried to endure its force. Even with the fury of a winter storm beating at her door, Elizabeth had never felt so safe and so very happy. She did not know what tomorrow would hold, but she was intimately acquainted with the One who held tomorrow. That knowledge caused goose bumps of excitement to run up and down her spine. She knew He had a plan for her life, and she was finally learning to just rest in His arms and allow Him to bring it to pass. She knew there had been many times in her life that she had chosen to rely on some*one* or some*thing* other than God, and she had learned how foolish that could be. She vividly remembered the day that she had come to the end of herself and released everything to Him. She had laid her Isaac down. Now there was no way to fully explain the peace that she was experiencing from resting in His arms.

Looking across the room, Elizabeth wondered why she hadn't turned on the gas fireplace. She just couldn't get used to the idea of being able to enjoy a fire without the mess. Knowing that she had plenty of time to unpack and straighten up, she decided to light the logs and make this the most leisurely lunch hour on record.

She had almost finished eating when she realized that she had let her mind drift so that she was almost in a dream state. She had been so busy for the past few weeks that she had written very little in her journal. That journal had so often been her avenue of therapy, her release, her healing balm. She would take a few minutes to record at least these past two days. Of course, she wouldn't have proper words to describe the beauty around her on this mountain, the love in the eyes of the Jamisons or the peace deep within her own heart, but she would write something. After all, she would be the only one to ever read the journal, and when she did she knew the memories would be vivid to her.

Tears flowed uncontrollably as Elizabeth read page after page in the worn old book that was her life.

"I will not do this," she hissed aloud. "The past is just that—the past! The only thing it is good for is to see how good God has always been to me—even in the worst of times. He was always there preparing me, protecting me, loving me. I am not going to let what could have been, what should have been, keep me from what now is!"

REFLECTION AND DIRECTION

She knew that the reading of that journal would unravel the mystery of her present life for anyone who read it. But there was no real mystery, no hidden secret that caused her to be intriguing or sinister or strange. Her's was simply a life that was all too ordinary, all too real. In its simplicity, there was also a tangled web of complexities that she had been too naïve—no, too afraid—to delve into. Then the coverings had been abruptly, rudely, cruelly ripped off, revealing the stench of putrid, festering sores that might never heal. Her life had been inextricably changed ... and she had not been given any choice in the matter.

Laying the journal aside, Elizabeth rose from her chair. Walking slowly to the piano, she allowed her fingers to lovingly, tenderly touch the keys as one might caress the soft flesh of a newborn baby or that of an aged saint.

"I can't bring music from you," she said wistfully. "But you're here ... waiting; someday ... someone will. You'll resonate with melodious tunes again ... someday ... as you did ... before." With that, she smiled. That thought often brought tears, but not today. God was continuing to wipe tears away and in their places, a smile.

She slowly walked back to the fireplace and looked up into the old mirror. Once again she made jokes about her plainness.

"Well, girl," she said aloud. "Those whisperers in town were not wrong. You are a bit long in the tooth for such a venture—and alone, no less. Even with highlights, that hair is still dry, frizzled, and mousy. Those glasses keep sliding down your very prominent nose, and those store-bought teeth have started clacking when you talk. Yes, you have definitely seen your better days—long ago. Shouldn't you really be looking for a rest home instead of a business license? Or maybe it's an insane asylum you need!"

As she laughed and turned from the mirror, Elizabeth began to reflect on what had brought her to this place. After all, she was almost sixty years old, much too old by anyone's calculations to be starting out on her own, by herself, in uncharted waters. The only answer that kept coming to her as she asked herself that question was from the book of Samuel where God said concerning Joseph, "What the devil saw for evil, God saw for good."

That was the only answer she had, for the pain that had been inflicted on her was certainly and most surely from the pit of hell. She felt as if she could now better understand some of the pain of the Psalmist when he spoke of being utterly cast down—encompassed about by evil, so close to absolute despair. But God was there, had been there all along. She had entreated Him for answers and for help, and He had picked her up, held her in His arms, given her strength, and then just at the right time—had sent her out.

Yes, she did feel too old. She was all alone, and she was scared. But what else was she to do? Aren't all situations and all events and all circumstances in the hands of an omnipotent and omniscient God? Aren't the steps of His children ordered by

Him? Isn't it up to Him to bring to fruition that which He has planned? Her heart sang all the answers: "Yes! Yes! Yes!" Then wouldn't it have been an act of disobedience not to follow His leadership even in a matter like this? She tried to remember the ages of Abraham and Moses and Noah and the ridicule and jeers they encountered on their journeys. Elizabeth knew in her heart that she was in the perfect will of God, so she would just leave the rest up to Him. He had done right by her thus far, and now she found herself getting excited about the next step!

As she turned once more to view the scene outside her window, she thought again of that cold January day five years before. She moved closer to the fireplace as a shiver went up her spine, knowing full well it was not the cold that placed it there. She had found them there … together … Martin and Vera … in her home. Vera had come there to discuss some business venture with him—and he was just comforting her in a time of personal difficulty. He had ended it with Vera before—or at least that's what he had told Elizabeth. But she knew it had not ceased in frequency or intensity—and now he was telling her he had made his choice. He had no more need or use for Elizabeth, their marriage, or their family. It was over!

Just that easily and simply he was ending their thirty-five-year marriage. He had always been the breadwinner and Elizabeth a dependent wife. Although his job required long hours and frequent trips out of town, he seemed quite happy. It was only in the last couple of years that his trips had become more frequent and of longer duration. He had become more moody and was generally unconcerned about things at home. Elizabeth had become a master of rationalization, so she just passed this off as another normal, though unpleasant occurrence in a marriage of long standing. Down deep, she *must* have known better, but what was she to do?

When Martin made the ridiculous decision to destroy their home and marriage, Elizabeth was devastated, but her deep faith in God had carried her through. By her own admission, it was the longest, darkest tunnel she had ever traveled through. She couldn't even support herself. After all, she was a housewife, more than fifty years old, with her greatest assets being her domestication skills. In order to sustain life, she left her home, went back to the small town of her birth, and started helping to restore and operate a country inn.

It took a long time for healing to begin. Each time she felt some sense of recovery, more wounds were inflicted, but finally she began to see a glimmer of hope. She lived on such meager fare that depression overtook her to the point that for some time she was forced to be under a doctor's care.

Her life with Martin had been far from perfect, but she had made the best of it. She made do with whatever she had and tried her best to keep their friends from knowing the pain and indignities she suffered.

It seemed that the day would never come when there would be real closure on her life with Martin. He had quickly filed for a divorce, and it was granted. There was nothing she could do to stop it. He was ordered to pay her a few dollars as support until final property settlement was made. About the only thing that the money provided was payment for her beloved piano, but at least she was warm and fed at the inn, so she survived.

After many times of postponement, the settlement finally took place. As Elizabeth knew would be the case, the lawyers seemed to be the big winners. She even allowed Martin to buy out her share of the real estate, which wasn't much. The house was in such need of repair and would require so much upkeep, she knew she couldn't begin to do it, and there was still a loan against it that she couldn't pay. She had been born poor, raised poor, and lived poor, but even with the settlement money in her hand she had never felt so destitute. The only thing that kept her going was the knowledge that God had built worldwide ministries on pennies, so she bowed her head and dedicated every cent to Him.

Because Elizabeth Barrington had built her life on the truth of God's Word and always covered her most painful problems with prayer, she was already being given direction for the next phrase of her life. She had prayerfully been seeking God's face and His guidance from the day this nightmare had begun, so when the courts closed that chapter of her life, she was already receiving direction for the next. In her own strength and in her own mind she had tried to pursue several options. Each time she tried to put her ideas before the Lord she would receive a resounding. "No, my child, not yet, not that way."

When the idea of a bed and breakfast in the Blue Ridge Mountains came up she did not know what to think. From where had that idea come? She prayed and entreated God many, many times and kept getting the same answer. She didn't understand anything more than she was to take some time and travel north across the North Carolina line into Virginia. She wasn't to go to a large metropolitan area but to a small town, but she had no idea which one.

Not really knowing where to begin, Elizabeth decided to go to the library and use their computer to look up some information about southwestern Virginia. That within itself had been a giant, bold step into the unknown. She had never even turned on a computer. The librarian was very helpful, so without any problem, she was soon checking out the area. Not receiving any definitive direction that first day, she continued to pray and search. When she eventually hooked up with a realtor in a little, obscure town, she went home more confused than ever. A few days later the realtor called to say she wanted to fax her some information that she thought might be of help.

There were several properties that looked promising, but they were much too expensive. The ones that she thought might be in her price range were either very old and dilapidated, or they were right in the middle of the tiny town. She knew God had directed her away from both those situations, so she gracefully told the realtor she didn't find anything that she thought would work. She was bewildered when the realtor faxed her back almost immediately. She had sent pages and pages of listings.

"If you can come next week," the fax had stated, "I've a place for you to stay. I'll take you around to these places. That way you'll be able to see them up close and personal."

She knew she was to go, so she set it up.

The Search

Pulling into the realtor's office was daunting to Elizabeth, so she breathed a prayer—again, asking for a calm spirit, for clarity of mind, and for indisputable direction. This was definitely a first for her. There had been lots of those lately, and only God knew how many more there were to be. On entering the office, she was greeted immediately by an attractive woman with the most gorgeous mop of red hair she had ever seen.

"You must be Elizabeth Barrington," said the woman warmly. "You are exactly what I pictured you to be. Your voice matches you perfectly. That's seldom the case, don't you know. But with you, yes, indeedy, I would have known you anywhere! Oh my, I haven't even introduced myself, but I'm just so glad to be meeting you after all our calls and faxes. Aren't those fax machines something? I'm glad now that they insisted I get one. I'm Adele. I feel like I've known you forever. Here, sit yourself down. Want some coffee? I bet you drove straight up here from North Carolina this morning, didn't you? And it's not just a little past ten o'clock. You must have left way before dawn!" With that she pulled out a chair for Elizabeth and handed her a big mug of coffee.

"I bet you'd prefer tea, wouldn't you?" she went on. "You just look like a tea drinker. But you'll have to learn to like coffee if you and I are going to be buds. I keep the coffee companies in business, don't you know."

She laughed the warmest, most infectious laugh that Elizabeth had heard in many a day. This delightful, bubbly woman put Elizabeth completely at ease, and she knew right then that Adele was someone she wanted to be "buds" with.

"Oh, this is great. I drink lots of coffee too, especially in the morning. Later in the day it's usually tea, but this is just what I need right now. And might I add, this is an excellent cup of coffee. Is it a special blend?"

"No," Adele said, laughing. "No special blend, not even a special brand. I just got a little secret when it comes to making coffee. I'll share it with you some day, but you'll have to share some secret of yours with me, don't you know." She gave Elizabeth a pat on the shoulder and went back around the chair to her desk.

"Now, let's get started here," she stated in a voice that was so professional and yet so warm and friendly Elizabeth was amazed. She felt a real witness of the Spirit with this woman.

"I've lined up quite a few places that I want to show you, but I've had a meeting come up unexpectedly, so I'm afraid I won't be free until lunchtime. If it's okay with you, I'll just take you on over to the parsonage and you can get settled in. I'll get freed up just as soon as possible and come back for you. I really am sorry. I hope this won't be too much of an inconvenience for you."

Elizabeth could feel the depth of the woman's apology. This person was genuine; she was real, and Elizabeth knew she could put away all her preconceived doubts and fears about "real estate barracudas." This lady was not one of those.

"No, no. That's just fine," she said quickly. "No inconvenience at all. I have been in the car since very early, and I've got major fanny fatigue. It will be a relief just to walk around a bit. I just realized when I stopped out front that I hadn't been out of that car in over four hours. That wasn't very smart, was it? I guess I was more anxious to get here than I thought."

"Oh, honey. I'm sure you are travel weary. Fanny fatigue! I like that one! For me, that would be a lot of fatigue, don't you know!" She laughed again so genuinely that Elizabeth couldn't help joining in.

"Well, you're here now, and I'm going to take good care of you. Come on, let's go meet Preacher Bill and Sister Carol. They're really looking forward to meeting you. You're going to love them to death; they just don't come any better. If I know Carol she'll have a fresh buttermilk pound cake waiting ... and now Carol, she'll have tea ... tea of all kinds. She'll fix you right up. You know how it is with preachers' wives; she's got to be ready to be hospitable to anybody and everybody at all times. And if there's anything that Carol is, it's hospitable. She's just got the gift, don't you know. She can wipe away tears, banish fears, and give a mouse the courage to stand up to a crouching cat. Honey, she's wonderful." On she went.

"Oh, and Preacher Bill, he's great, too. Preaches the Bible straight and true—he'll stand by the Word, no matter what. I've seen him face opposition that would cause most men to tuck tail and run—and he's just a boy, don't you know. But Bill, oh no, he just keeps standing, and God has honored him for it. He has single-handed, with God's help of course, closed liquor joints and run gamblers out of this town. Why, I think even the druggies are afraid to come around here for fear that Bill will call up God to wipe 'em out, don't you know. Yeah, Bill and Carol, they're the best."

All the while Adele had been ushering Elizabeth outside. With a friendly wave she headed to her car.

"Follow me, honey. We're just a hop, skip, and a jump away."

Elizabeth turned to follow Adele's Jeep Cherokee out onto the main street that ran through town. She was smiling as she tried to absorb all that she had just heard and seen. She still didn't know what lay ahead; but she did know that she felt great peace and excitement at the same time.

She had always known that following God by faith was the only way to go. You never know what is around the next corner, over the next hill, inside the next door, but you can always know that it is going to be the best for you, and your acceptance of it will bring glory to God.

What more could anyone ever want? Neither fame, nor fortune, nor prestige could bring to any person what the peace of God could. His leadership, help, and strength were all she desired, and her abiding faith in Him caused her to know she already had all of that.

At the red light on Main Street Adele turned left, went about the distance of two city blocks, and turned left again. There in front of them, just off to the right, was the First Baptist Church of Leesboro. How wonderful to have the church within walking distance of town itself. It was obviously an old church, but it was beautiful. It was dark red brick with a sweeping porch and stately two-story pillars. A wide walk curved from the parking lot to the steps. At either end of the porch tastefully designed handicap access ramps had been added, making the whole front look so inviting to anyone who would care to enter. It looked as if every patch of earth that was not paved had some flowering shrub or bush or tree planted in it. She had not, on the entire trip from North Carolina, seen anything so impressive. It was not ostentatious at all; it just simply stood as a silent monument to the love that went into even the upkeep of the place. It was obvious, too, that it took more than just one pair of hands to do the job.

Surely a group of God's people had worked together to care for their building and these grounds—and that spoke volumes to her. Doesn't the façade say a lot about the inside? She knew that had been true in many other cases. This was definitely a place she wanted to visit. Was it possible that God was so easily showing her a new place to worship and serve?

Open Doors

Going on past the church, they stopped in front of a small but equally well-kept red brick house, perfectly matching the church. Late summer flowers and hanging baskets of ferns, geraniums, and impatiens were everywhere. An inviting porch swing and two big old oak rockers seemed to be waiting, inviting some weary soul to occupy them. How many problems had been solved right here by God's man listening with a heart of love and then speaking with wisdom gleaned from hours in the Word and on his knees? Sermons from pulpits were very important tools used by God, but Elizabeth thought that rocking chairs and porch swings and shoulders to cry on were invaluable as well.

Before the car engines were quieted, a lovely young woman was hurrying across the porch and down the steps to greet them. *She is stunning*, thought Elizabeth. She wasn't sure what she had expected but apparently not such a young and beautiful lady. It was almost disconcerting to her. This entire community was becoming one big question mark to her. Should she approach with a heightened level of caution? She knew God loved her and wanted to give her His best, but she was really being overwhelmed.

"Adele, good morning." The young woman's voice literally rang out like music when she spoke. Her manner was so easy as she unashamedly hugged first Adele and then Elizabeth. "And this has to be Ms. Barrington. Welcome to Leesboro and to my home. Please come in. I've just put the kettle on and taken a cake out of the oven."

"See what I told you, Elizabeth," Adele said in such a way that she could just feel the love the older woman had for the younger. "I think this girl has little angel-elves around who produce those cakes for her. I wish you'd consider these thunder thighs of mine, young lady, and just serve fruit and rice cakes instead."

Carol laughed and started to say something, but before she could, Adele went on. "Don't you dare, girl, unless you want to see me get arrested for creating murder and mayhem around here. Out of my way! Let me at that cake!" From the way both of them laughed, she knew this must have been a running joke with them for years. The aroma was drawing them into the sun-filled kitchen where the teakettle was now whistling a merry tune.

"Where's Preacher Bill?" Adele asked. "Doesn't he have the nose of a bloodhound when that cake is ready?"

Carol's countenance fell, and Elizabeth was sure tears were welling in those big blue eyes. "He got a call just before you got here about Granny Richards. We'd been expecting it, but you're never really prepared. She was asking for him, and I've been praying he'd get there before ..." Her voice trailed off, and she turned away. Adele quickly picked up the conversation.

"Oh, I am so sorry to hear that, but we have all been expecting it. We mustn't be sad, though. This is what she has been looking forward to for a long time. She has been saying for several weeks now that surely her coronation day would come soon. The angels are rejoicing around the throne at her homecoming, don't you know!"

Carol quickly composed herself and turned back to serve each of them a generous slice of warm pound cake. Realizing Elizabeth didn't know what they were talking about, Carol sat down and with a faraway look in her eyes began to explain.

"Ms. Barrington, Granny Richards was ninety-one years old, the oldest member of our congregation and the first person to invite Bill and me to her home when we came here seven years ago. She lived way up in Windy Gap and probably had the least, materially speaking, of anyone I've ever known. But I believe every prayer that dear lady ever prayed went directly to the throne room of God and touched His heart. Truly, our tears at her passing are not for her but for those of us who will have to figure out a way to go on without her. I just hope and pray that I have learned a little of what she attempted to teach me and that I might be able to touch some life the way she has touched all of ours."

The little kitchen was quiet for some time as three Christian women sat reverently observing a time of respect for the dear old saint. The loud whistling of the teakettle jarred them from their spiritual reverie.

"Oh, dear," Carol said apologetically as she hurried to the stove. "I forgot your tea. What kind would you like, Ms. Barrington? Here's a tray of herbals and one of regulars." She pushed the tray toward Elizabeth, who selected Lemon Zinger. As if reading her mind, Carol set the honey bear in front of her.

"Please call me Elizabeth, dear. Ms. Barrington sounds so formal, and I like to be informal with special friends whenever I can." This lovely young woman had already moved into a daughter-room in Elizabeth's heart bringing a mixture of emotions, both happy and sad.

"None for me, sweetie," Adele said as she rose from her chair and reached for a paper towel and began to wrap her cake. "I'm going to be late for that silly meeting if I don't scoot out of here, but I am not going to leave my cake behind. Now, Elizabeth, I'll be back about a quarter to one. I'll introduce you to Dot and Floyd at The Diner, and we'll head out from there. You rest a bit 'cause I'll probably talk ya and walk ya to death this afternoon, don't you know!" She gave Carol a big motherly hug and sped away, a gal on a mission.

What a character, Elizabeth mused. *If there is a place here for me, I'm sure she will help me find it. Lord, I still don't understand your bringing me here, but I sure do hope you have a place for me. How could a place I've never been or even heard of feel like home?* She had so many questions and right now very few answers.

Carol showed her on back to the guest room where she was to stay while in Leesboro. She would never have expected to have a realtor look out for her lodging, and to find that she was to stay at the preacher's house free of charge was just more than she could comprehend. She knew all of this had been set in motion by the God of the universe so she could not—would not—look on it as charity. This was a lesson she was having great difficulty learning, but situations of the recent past had been diligently teaching her. She had never had any problem at all with giving; she had always been charitable, often giving her last dollar or her most-prized possession. The receiving was where the rub came. She knew there were spiritual truths about the humility involved in accepting help or things or whatever, but she knew also that she had not yet arrived there.

She took her bags in while Carol was on the phone with someone, telling them that Granny Richards had just passed away. Preacher Bill came in and went immediately to hold his dear wife and privately talk and pray with her. Elizabeth chose not to encroach on this private moment. She waited until he was gone and then went out to bring in some things from her car. As she went back and forth, she overhead bits and pieces of the phone conversation. Carol was saying how greatly relieved she had been to find that her husband hadn't been too late and that she had come to terms with the old lady's passing. Elizabeth heard her say to the person on the phone that she didn't know enough about the issue to discuss it, but she would mention it to Bill and that she knew the Lord would direct.

After hanging up the phone, she came to see if Elizabeth needed anything and then told her she would let her rest until Adele came for her. Elizabeth thanked her, and after hanging some things in the closet, she decided that she would lie down for just a minute or two. She had gotten up really early, and although she loved traveling, she was always somewhat tense on a trip alone. In a very short time, she was settled comfortably on the big bed with its handcrafted quilt coverlet. As she drifted off, she wondered how many of God's servants had lifted up prayers for this sleepy little community from this very place. What she didn't know was that she was to play a very important role in the answer to some of those *effectual, fervent prayers* of days in the recent past.

The little travel clock that she had set for 11:30 jangled loudly, jarring her awake. She jumped up quickly, hardly believing she had been in such deep sleep. It took her a couple of minutes to realize where she was. She hurriedly dressed in jeans and a loose denim shirt. She had decided on boots and a hat, not knowing what Adele might have in store for her. She grabbed her purse and was just coming out of the room when she heard Carol speaking to Adele.

"She's been resting, but I'll go get her."

"Here I am, all rested, ready, and raring to go."

Both ladies laughed, and again Elizabeth felt an ease she hardly ever felt with anyone. Just then Preacher Bill came in, and proper introductions were made. He was a dashing young man, tall, athletic, and dignified looking even in his faded jeans and

T-shirt. He wore Reeboks and a Braves cap, and she thought he would have looked more at home on a college campus—or a movie set—than here.

"We must be off, Preacher, but don't eat all that cake. We'll be back." Adele waved a friendly good-bye, closed Elizabeth's door, and off they went. She looked back to see the young pastor gather his bride in his arms, and she knew they were still weeping for Granny Richards.

Feeling sure that Adele had an agenda well in hand, she just sat back and enjoyed the short ride back into town. As they entered the quaint little diner, she quickly surveyed every inch of the place. It was spotless, and the aroma of burger and fries carried her back to days of long ago. It seemed that every booth and every table was occupied, but Dottie must have been expecting them.

"Here you go, ladies, best seat in the house. Hey, there. I'm Dottie. That good-looking hunk of a fry cook over there's Floyd. And I know you're Ms. Barrington. Glad to meet ya. I can tell already you're goin' to like to here. We ain't big and uptown, and we ain't high faluting neither. Set ya self down. What kin I get ya? The usual, Adele?"

It took a great deal of will power for Elizabeth to remain composed. She wasn't upset really, but how on earth did everybody in town already know her? And what did they know? She hadn't told Adele much about herself, but these people acted as if she were some favorite relative returning from a faraway place. And why didn't that upset her? She was by nature a very private person, usually remaining behind a strong, impenetrable curtain. Here it didn't bother her at all though, and she was bewildered to say the least.

As she looked around the room, she wondered if this was the only eating establishment in town. It certainly looked as if the entire population was crammed into this tiny place, but she knew she had seen a steak house and a burger joint or two and even a pizza parlor on her way in. As she saw some of the plates being delivered to the tables, the answer to that question became crystal clear. Not only were the portions abundant and the aroma mesmerizing, but the food was also beautifully presented. This might be a small-town diner, but it was no greasy spoon. She half expected to see Emeril LaGasse or Julia Child wave to them from the kitchen. Not being sure, she had let Adele order for her, but next time she would not hesitate to order anything on the menu. She had eaten many a hamburger in her day, but none compared to this.

Several people came by to speak, make small talk with Adele, and welcome "Ms. Barrington" to town. They acted as if she were already a bona fide resident, and she hadn't even seen a single piece of property yet. She was beginning to feel as she would be letting the town down and condemning herself to a fate worse than death if she didn't come here to live. She kept thinking she would awaken from this weird dream any minute now.

"Guess we'd better be on our way, honey. You may need to see lots of places before you decide on one, don't you know. I know we'll find a place for you; it's just a matter of which one."

Elizabeth nodded agreement to Adele and reached for the check. Adele jerked it away so swiftly it almost startled Elizabeth. She wouldn't hear to having her guest pick up the bill. A guest in this town was just that, a guest, with all the rights and privileges. She laughed that warm, familiar laugh that Elizabeth had already grown to love, paid Dottie, and escorted her out the door. Everybody in the place yelled bye and said they'd see her later.

Adele, clattering a mile a minute, wheeled out of the parking space and down to the intersection that led north out of town. She told Elizabeth about a place that had just gone on the market. She thought it might be just the ticket. It was a little pricey, but she thought she might be able to talk the owner down a bit. If necessary, a mortgage could be obtained, with the rentals probably making the payments.

Elizabeth felt her stomach go queasy—and not from the lunch. She hadn't explained everything to Adele, but she knew God did not intend her to take on a mortgage. That question had been settled at the onset. When God had started her on this quest, she was quick to remind Him of her limited funds and that nothing could be purchased for that amount of money. He had, with great certainty, assured her that there was a place for her to buy … without a mortgage.

Defying Darkness

Soon they were pulling off the highway and starting down a winding, narrow, country road. Unkempt fields lay on either side. Scrub pines shot up all over the place. There was an uncomfortable sense of oppression and foreboding all around. Elizabeth felt an urgent need of entering into an attitude of prayer. She sat quietly, watching Adele, who had also gone uncharacteristically quiet.

Eventually, the road straightened, and before them in the distance she could see a building, looming up as if out of the very ground. It was very large and not nearly as dismal looking as the first glimpse had seemed. As a matter of fact, she could see some potential there, but it just didn't feel right for her.

As they pulled up in front, they saw two women sitting in a gazebo over in the side yard. The younger of the two quickly made her way across the yard and met them as they got out of the car. She was not really discourteous as she greeted them, but it was quite obvious she intended for their visit to be a short one.

Adele, recognizing the young woman as the granddaughter of the older one, introduced Elizabeth and stated their business. By now the older woman had joined them, and much to the chagrin of the younger, she had offered them refreshments.

Adele thanked her and told her they had just eaten and that they wouldn't be staying long this time.

"I was just explaining to Mrs. Curry that the property has already been sold, Grandmother."

"Yes, that's mostly right, Adele. Come on over here, and I'll tell you all about it." They moved out of Elizabeth's range of hearing, so she just tried to make small talk with Marcie. She was a pretty girl, and much younger than she had first appeared. She kept flashing disapproving looks in the direction of her grandmother and Adele. When they started back toward the car, she seemed greatly relieved. This visit had been about as welcome as an IRS audit.

The old lady chatted on for a few more minutes. Adele hugged her good-bye after promising to come back to visit soon. Marcie bid a curt farewell and quickly guided her grandmother into the house. Elizabeth was never so happy to be leaving a place. She waited for Adele to open the conversation.

"I could tell you weren't interested in that one anyway, were you, dear?"

"Not at all! I've never felt so much oppression in my life. What is wrong with that place?"

Adele remained silent as she skillfully maneuvered the Jeep up the washed-out road. When she spoke, it was with carefully chosen words.

"That young woman there, Marcie—she's known her share of problems and dealt with her own set of demons. It's common knowledge that she has turned her back on God and everything holy. She's living in all kinds of ungodliness down there in Atlanta; probably only here now to get Miss Bea's money and Miss Bea knows it.

"But Bea's a sharp old Steel Magnolia. The girl doesn't know that she has that land so tied up legally; they'll both be dead and gone long before it gets untangled. Even then the girl won't get the money. Miss Bea let the girl think she was going along with her scheme but just so she would let her guard down.

"The authorities are already working on a plan; they'll be here to pick Marcie up before she knows what has happened to her. That girl is full of the devil. That's where the oppression comes from.

"I'm glad they're going to get her away from Miss Bea. I wouldn't trust her as far as I could throw a bull by the horns. I'm glad we came down here though, even if it's not the right place for you. A least I got to check on Miss Bea, and with two of God's children in this car and one on the ground that little devil girl didn't stand a chance. Just you hide and watch what Miss Bea has up her sleeve. The Lord be praised!"

They were back on the highway now, and for some strange reason Elizabeth wasn't at all upset that Adele had taken her there. She even felt that perhaps God had used her to help Adele and Miss Bea do battle with the devil, and that together they had won. Obviously, Leesboro was not exempt from attacks by the forces of evil, but here, too, God would give victory to and through His servants.

"Let's move on to property number two now, girl. Don't look so concerned; we've only begun to travel." Adele reached over and patted her hand and that big Ipana smile dashed her fears right out the window. She found herself wanting to hear all the stories this woman could tell. She most assuredly was not a half-empty glass sort of person. She probably ripped the gray from the clouds and sewed the silver linings in herself.

They next went up a street just off Main that led toward the medical center. Adele had only yesterday gotten word that a place on that street was going on the market. She hadn't even talked with anybody about it yet, and she knew it was awfully close in, but it wouldn't hurt to look.

As with most small towns, you could go around the corner from the municipal buildings and find yourself in a different world. That certainly held true here. Adele pointed out the house just up ahead, and Elizabeth could see that it was at least pretty nearly the size she was envisioning, but that was about all it had going for it. Just up the road and very visible was an unkempt trailer park, of all things, and across from that a manufacturing plant of some sort. Need she ask of city zoning or proper land use management? The house itself Adele said sat on about three quarters of an acre, and just some basic landscaping would make a world of difference.

"Just mowing the lawn and picking up the garbage would make a world of difference," she moaned. "Oh, Adele, I don't mean to be ugly, and I am so grateful for all your help, but this is terrible."

"Yes, yes it is. Let's get out of this depressing place. But let me at least show you how to get in to the medical center since we're so close. Can't ever tell when you might need it. It's just right up here."

The sight of the center with its impressive grounds picked her spirits up.

"The main building is pre Civil War," Adele was saying, "but the wings were added only about four years ago. We have a fine staff of EMS people, and a new surgeon has just recently accepted a position here."

Adele was on the board, and Elizabeth could sense the feeling of pride as she laid out every detail of the establishment. It was comforting to know that the wonderful people of this little town did have some of the outside world at work for them.

"I know we have not done too well today, Elizabeth," Adele's voice again had that firm professional but friendly quality, "but this is only our first day. We don't get defeated this easily, not in Leesboro. I'm going to take you back. Tonight is prayer meeting, and I'm sure you'll want to go."

Even if she had not planned to go with them to church this first night, the matter was already pretty much settled. Adele dropped her off at the parsonage, waiting only long enough to see Carol at the door, yelled, "See ya after while," and roared away.

Carol, with the perception of a seasoned hostess, served Elizabeth some of her soothing peppermint tea. They chatted briefly about the disappointments of the day. Elizabeth excused herself to rest and freshen up for the evening service. She had persuaded Carol to allow her to come back in and help prepare supper. She had already learned that the preacher was especially fond of potato cakes and coleslaw, and Elizabeth wagered she could make them the way his grandma had.

The developing relationship with these two precious young people brought to mind the words of Proverbs 17:22: "A merry heart doeth good like a medicine." The easy manner in which they had opened their hearts and home to her was refreshing. Maybe she really could be on the way to trusting again. The crushed spirit that had been caused by her debilitating circumstances had been a part of her life for too long. She dropped to her knees beside the bed, and there in the privacy of a strange new world, she poured out her heart to God.

After a long soak in the tub, she went in to help Carol in the kitchen. They talked about Carol's family in Newport News. Her dad was a retired navy man, and her mom had been a stay-at-home wife and mother.

"My mom and dad would have celebrated their thirty-fifth anniversary this year ..." Her voice trailed as she turned away.

Elizabeth respected her silence and embraced it. It was as if each knew the other was feeling too much pain to continue. They were both visibly relieved when Bill came bounding in. He pecked Carol on the cheek, patted Elizabeth on the shoulder, and immediately went about what must have been his normal routine of setting the table, babbling all the while about how he was hungry enough to eat a horse.

She felt so much a part of this home, this town, and these people, but she knew she did not yet really belong. Not just because she had found no house but because her heart, spirit, and soul had not yet caught up to where they all were. She was nearly twice as old as Carol and Bill, but they were light years ahead of her in life.

Bill raved about the supper, emptying every bowl as a teenager would after a sporting event. This time, he planted kisses on the heads of both women and then somewhat sheepishly made his exit and headed toward the church. Carol caught the wistful look in Elizabeth's eye and felt a wave of sadness flow over her. As if by some divine revelation, she sensed the deep pain in the older woman and determined in her soul to be a vessel available to help alleviate that pain.

They cleared the table, put the dishes in the dishwasher, and left the little house together, Bibles in hand for the evening service. This they did as easily as if from years of routine. A bond that neither understood nor even thought about was being forged between them—a bond that in days to come would prove immensely important to both.

As they walked toward the church, Elizabeth could see that the parking lot was full. It looked more like the gathering for Sunday morning instead of Wednesday night. What a refreshing sight. Was this what Norman Rockwell's creative eye had seen for one of his beautiful renderings of Americana? The backdrop of the Blue Ridge Mountains literally glowed in the late afternoon sun. Back home summer was still searing the countryside, but here autumn was poised, ready to burst on the scene in all its glory. The hills truly were alive with His majesty and glory. And yes, with the sound of music, too. From inside the church songs of praise were ringing out into the hills.

Exchanging greetings with other worshipers, they walked up the massive steps. Elizabeth caught sight of a beautifully hand scripted plaque just to the left of the huge double doors. She was compelled to stop and read it. What a work of art!

FIRST BAPTIST CHURCH OF LEESBORO
**ESTABLISHED AND DEDICATED TO OUR GOD
ON THIS DAY
SUNDAY JULY 1, 1863**

Below in smaller script were seven surnames:

**LEE, CURRY, JEFFERSON, PHILLIPS,
DAVIS, JAMISON, AND RICHARDS**

Elizabeth was trying to absorb all this when Carol spoke.

"A beautiful plaque, isn't it? It was done by Mr. Abel Phillips, the man who donated the property for the church. They say it took him almost four months to complete it, and he passed away two days after it was hung. You've probably already met some descendants of those families. You've heard of 'Old South Money'? Well, here we have 'Old South Religion.'" She laughed as they linked arms and entered the sanctuary.

Inside, Elizabeth allowed her eyes to soak up all the beauty of the old building—soaring stained glass windows and ceilings so high she had to lean her head back as far as it would go in order to see them. The wide, honey oak cove moldings literally shone. Years of life in this wonderful place had only enriched their beauty. The choir loft had been built higher than she was accustomed to. She couldn't help wondering if that helped the voices ring out more melodiously. Behind it was the baptistery with a huge cross rising above it. On the left was an antique grand piano; on the right, a rather ordinary, howbeit, modern organ, looked almost out of place. But the melodies coming from it were neither ordinary nor out of place. The young woman playing it had entered a world of her own. It was hard to tell where the instrument ended and the person began. Over the years, Elizabeth had been privileged to hear some renowned musicians play some priceless instruments, but few compared to this.

She quietly slipped onto the polished oak pew beside Carol, still mesmerized by all around her. She felt as if she had been whisked into a time warp when she entered this town. Her head was spinning to the extent that she half expected to see Alice and a huge white rabbit or maybe Dorothy and Toto. At the same time, she had never known such peace and contentment. The only thing she did know "for sure and for certain," as her grandmother would have said, was that she didn't want any of it to end.

As the choir ended with a rousing chorus of "Victory in Jesus" the entire building reverberated with "Amens!" Immediately, everyone began a ritual of hand shaking, back patting, neck hugging welcomes. Elizabeth smiled and accepted all the friendly gestures from the folks around her, but she didn't mix and mingle as the "regulars" were doing. Not that she objected; she was just still trying to absorb it all. There must have been more than a hundred people in this place— from infants and toddlers to teenage boys and girls, to young adults and aged grandparents;

and they were all having a great time. Had they never heard of the generation gap?

In the most leisurely manner on earth, the congregation took their places, and the young pastor stepped to the podium. As before, Carol sensed the pain that Elizabeth thought she had so completely concealed. Elizabeth fastened her eyes on the young man and felt the quickening heart only a mother could feel. Realism had arrested her thoughts, transporting her back to another place, another time—another place and time that had given her great joy but now only served to torment her days and soak her pillow at night. Only by keeping those thoughts locked away as valuables in a vault ... *or death in a coffin* ... could she go on.

Feeling much like a frail little ship reeling and rocking on a storm-tossed sea, she fought to compose herself. She glanced around to see if others had observed her disheveled state. Feeling confident that they had not, she straightened herself in her seat, smiled at a child in the left pew, and assumed her most dignified posture. She wasn't about to open her wounds of pain and confusion all over these people. She'd keep *that* to herself, even from God if she could. She had been doing so much better—at least she had thought so until just this moment. Why here, here in this holy place, was she so consumed with pain?

As she watched Preacher Bill take his position behind the sacred desk, she thought how much older and more dignified he appeared from the boy who had been at the dinner table such a short time ago. The handsome young man she had only yesterday mistaken for a college athlete was now a wise minister of the gospel, ready to give his flock their food for the day. When he bowed and began to pray, she knew that he had spent many hours alone with God, and she knew that not only were these waiting parishioners going to be fed from God's bountiful table but so was she.

Elizabeth had said many times that she had heard some of the best preachers that God ever called—and some of the worst. She had known many who fed the people as with a spoon and some who just dumped it in the trough. This young man before her was spreading a table with the love of a parent administering healing medicine to an ailing child, and he was doing it with the skill or a surgeon, cutting out the disease without harming the tiny healthy cells. His people were feasting and being filled and being healed. He was dissecting the Psalms and examining them as if he had been the writer. But he was only providing the mouthpiece through which God was speaking. She surmised that he must have been teaching in the Psalms on Wednesday nights for some time now. He closed with the reading of Psalm 67:1: "God be merciful unto us, and bless us; and cause his face to shine upon us; Selah."

He exhorted them to prayerfully read and study and mediate on the entire chapter until next Wednesday and then return, expecting God to speak.

Not Yet

Thursday morning dawned cool and crisp, with a sky so blue it carried Elizabeth back to the days of her mother's clothesline hanging full with her brother's Chapel Hill "Carolina Blue" paraphernalia. She could see the tiny drops of dew still dancing on the azaleas and rhododendrons outside her window, and her nostalgia just wouldn't retreat. Her night had been a restless one, and there in the dark she had tried to convince herself that she just needed to go on back home. But when she finally fell asleep, it was with the knowledge that it was not time to do that—not just yet.

Adele was there at nine, just as she had said she would be. With coffee mugs and napkins full of Carol's steaming hot cinnamon buns, they were off. Elizabeth had made up some of her yeast dough last night after church and left Carol instructions for the buns. She had done a perfect job, and that was her first time, too. In her humble way, she told Adele that it was only because Elizabeth had done the real work.

Everything seemed to be so perfect as they started out, and they both just knew they would find the right piece of property today. The pastor had even lifted Elizabeth's silent request up to

God during prayer time at church last night. Although she had only lifted her hand and he had just nodded acknowledgment, Elizabeth was sure everybody there knew her request and prayed about it, too.

They went first one way out of town and then another. At one time all Elizabeth could see were rolling hills with cattle grazing as contentedly as if they had just been placed there to give serenity to the landscape. She has seen green hills before, but these were in a class all by themselves. The lush carpet of grass she would have expected in Kentucky, but not here. The Blue Ridge Mountains were not just majestic mountains but simple hills and pristine valleys, too. It would have been an act of desecration to build a house anywhere here and mar the beauty of this glorious place. How often had she spoken up for preserving the natural beauty of the mountains of her own home state? She had become enraged when it appeared that money-hungry people were going to do more road building through the unspoiled mountains. She secretly hoped this land would never change from the way it was at this very moment.

On into the mountains they drove, and Elizabeth knew they were getting farther out than she wanted, but the drive was so beautiful she felt as if she were worshiping. She looked at a place or two and fell in love with both, but still neither of them was *it*. She started to apologize to Adele for taking up so much of her time, but she was stopped midsentence.

"Now, don't you even go there, girl. First of all, this is what I do, all the time, day in and day out. I do it 'cause I love it. Second, I told God right after your first call that I'd be His wheels or whatever He needed me to be where you were concerned. Did I tell you that I wasn't even supposed to be in the office that day? We had decided to close for a few days while some repairs were being made on the roof.

"I'd gone down to Lucinda's to get a shampoo and afterward without even thinking, I just unlocked the door and in I went. I was standing there in the middle of that cold, dark office feeling like a complete idiot, hoping nobody had seen me go in. That's when your call came in. God set this thing in motion between us, don't you know. Now, I've got all my paperwork caught up. Now there's a real miracle for you. So you're stuck with me until we find what God has for you, whether you like it or not."

Elizabeth felt tears making ruts down her face, creating mascara puddles on her cheeks. She reached for a tissue and sponged them away as quickly and carefully as possible. For several minutes neither of them spoke. When the conversation did resume, it was of a completely different nature.

"Did anyone introduce you to Anna Louise last night?"

"No, I don't believe so. I met so many people, but I don't remember that name." She was so bad with names. She often feared that people saw her as being aloof or unfriendly with her deficient memory.

"Oh, you'd remember her. She was that angel at the organ." Adele beamed as she spoke. "Her mama and I were classmates back in school about a hundred years ago."

"My, no. I wasn't formally introduced to her but I did tell her how much I enjoyed the music. She's wonderful. Is she a professional?"

"No, but I bet she could be. She's just a very dedicated young woman who has no equal in these parts. She's a widow, don't you know, and only thirty years old. She and her two brothers live on their grandparents' place just out of town. Her brother, Doc, leads the choir."

"I met him; and the younger one, too. What's his name? But they didn't say anything about the sister," Elizabeth explained.

Something kept nagging at her, trying to make its way through a mass of mental cobwebs; but what was it? Then she remembered. Just after she had spoken to the young woman, she had seen her talking with the pastor. The conversation seemed intense, and she thought she had seen tears in the girl's eyes as the preacher hugged her good-bye. Come to think of it, both Carol and Preacher Bill had appeared rather pensive later, as if they were helping to shoulder some new heavy burden.

"The younger boy is Joe Bob, and he's a dear. They're all just the finest Christian people you'd ever want to meet. They've really been tried in the fire, and now they are pure gold. Brightest lights I've ever seen, all of 'em."

Obviously Joe Bob had been born with Down's syndrome, but he was so pleasant and polite it hadn't even registered with her until he walked away. She had met lots of genetically and physically *perfect* young men who could have learned a lot from him.

Adele was rattling on about how Doc and Anna Louise were Joe Bob's guardians, "But they have always told him he was their angel," she said. "You ought to hear him when he grabs Carol's hand and laughs, 'Here we go,' he says, 'guardian and angel!'"

By now they were coming back into town. Elizabeth was exhausted. Surely they must have seen every piece of property in the realtor's catalogue. Why had nothing turned up? There had been several places that she had thought were possibilities, but on closer look, none had been right. Maybe she was being too picky. She had often been told she had a prime rib appetite but a Spam pocketbook. Yet she knew this entire plan had been handed to her by God, and she would know the place He had for her when she saw it. She didn't figure she even had enough money to order Spam this time, so it was *all* up to God.

Adele assured her that there were more places to see, so they'd start fresh tomorrow. She hugged Adele and thanked her as graciously as she knew how. On entering the parsonage she saw a note addressed to her. *Had to run an errand. Be back as quickly as*

I can. Make yourself at home. You know where everything is. Bill's visiting at the hospital. Love, Carol.

She just couldn't get over it. These young people had taken her into their home and treated her like a favorite aunt ... now even leaving their door open for her. She could be some crazed, psychopathic serial killer for all they knew. Oh, those sweet, trusting children. What could she ever do for them to return their hospitality and friendship?

The mantle clock was striking six as Elizabeth curled up in the big easy chair to watch the news. She had showered and dressed in a comfortable, colorful caftan. She had taken the liberty of starting supper for Carol: parmesan chicken, green peas, a garden salad, and Texas yeast rolls. She had peeled some fresh peaches, covered them with sugar, and set them in the 'fridge to chill for dessert. She hoped she wasn't overstepping her boundaries, but it just felt like the right thing to do. Carol had welcomed her help last night, so surely it would be okay.

As she switched off the TV and went in to check on dinner, she heard a car in the drive. *What perfect timing,* she thought. *The chicken is almost done, and the rolls need only a couple more minutes to rise.* She greeted both Carol and the preacher as they entered together. She was trying to read the look on Carol's face when she grabbed her and squealed.

"What is that aroma?" Preacher Bill yelled. "Have I died and gone to heaven? Or is this just the prelude to the Marriage Supper of the Lamb?" He began lifting lids and sailing around the kitchen like a deranged madman.

"I take it then that it was okay that I started dinner? You said to make myself at home. Well, cooking is what I do."

"Okay? Okay that you started dinner! I'm going to have you canonized! I whined all the way home about it being so late and us all being so hungry. You're an answer to prayer, isn't she, Bill?"

"Boy, I'll say," he answered with that big, boyish grin. "Would you adopt us, please?"

They laughed and talked together while finishing dinner. Elizabeth rejoiced to see the two of them enjoying their meal. They told her about Bill's hospital visits and Carol's work with the literacy council.

"That's where I went this afternoon," Carol said. "I'm always home by four thirty, but today my silly old car died. It wouldn't hit a lick when I tried to start it. I called Bill at the hospital, but he couldn't leave until Miss Fannie came out of recovery and they were sure she was going to be okay. There I was stuck at the library and worrying about needing to be here starting supper. Boy, was that needless worry! But I did help little Jaime Barnes finish her literature homework. She's such a sweetheart and seems to always need a friend. Even with a dead car the afternoon turned out good, didn't it?"

Before Elizabeth could respond, Bill asked, "How 'bout your day, Ms. Elizabeth? Have any luck?"

"I'm afraid not, Preacher. But Adele keeps telling me not to worry; she's got more places to show me. I declare I think she may have to create some more land and build more houses overnight if she shows me any more tomorrow. I'm not sure, but I think we may have toured the entire state of Virginia today, and maybe a bit of West Virginia, too. I must admit I am beginning to get discouraged and weary. I'm not doubting God; I just want to be sure I have my ear attuned to His voice."

Both Bill and Carol tried to assure her that they too knew that in God's time He would bring to pass all that He had planned. How many times had she said those very same words of encouragement to others, and she knew they were true. She had seen God move in His time. She knew she must rest on His promise.

Continuing On

As Adele skillfully maneuvered the Jeep along first one country road and then another, Elizabeth scanned the landscape, hoping to see something that would speak to her. If she hadn't come here with a specific task to accomplish, she could have found this to be a most enjoyable tour. The air blowing softly through the half-opened window felt comforting to her skin, and the sweet fragrance of newly mown hay carried her back to another place, another time, another life. When they slowed to turn onto a side road, she could hear the sound of a rushing stream and the laughter of children. The two women had been enjoying each other's company, and she had been given quite a history lesson as Adele pointed out various properties and their inhabitants. She had a plethora of information on the area and loved sharing it. *If I ever write a book,* thought Elizabeth, *here's my first volume of reference.*

As they came nearer the creek, Adele slowed down and called to one of the picnickers. A well-tanned young man returned her greeting, walking toward Adele's car as they parked at the water's edge.

"Howdy, ladies. How ken I help ya?"

His speech so slow, his manner so calm, Elizabeth found herself thinking, *He's bound to be from Texas.* She was Southern, but this fellow could have had a mint julep in one hand, magnolias in the other, and be riding a Longhorn steer.

"Well, sir." Adele knew how to address an Ashley Wilkes when she saw one. "We just came out to see the old Jefferson place. I heard that somebody had made a bid on it. I guess you'd be that somebody, huh?"

"Yes, ma'am. That'd be me. Matthew Browning at your service." Elizabeth was sure if he had been wearing a Stetson he would have removed it and bowed to the ground.

"We just finalized all the paperwork yesterday, so I guess this is our day of frolickin' in celebration. Been trying to git my family up to these parts for years. We're tickled plumb to death to be here. Ya see, my granddaddy and ole Mr. Jefferson went way back, and my granddaddy and my daddy kept telling' me 'bout this place. They'd all be mighty proud, mighty proud indeed, to know I'm goin' be takin' up residence here. That pretty little red-haired filly over there is my wife Laura Lou, and them's my twin boys, Eddie Lee and Johnny Paul. They're ten. That little bitty slip of an angel doll, that's Jennie Sue; she's four. They're not always so unsociable; they're just 'fraid to quit playin'; 'fraid they'll wake up from this glorious dream."

Both women laughed, introduced themselves, and waved at the rambunctious gang in the creek. Somehow kids, creeks, and late summer days just said it all. From somewhere deep within, Elizabeth brought to mind one of Carl Sandburg's Chicago poems simply entitled "Happiness." He had seen a man, a field, and a family; here she was seeing the same truths being portrayed on an even more colorful canvas. They chatted briefly and then sent the young man back to join his blissful brood. Elizabeth had not even seen a house or the rest of the property, but it could never have been hers. In a long-ago plan it belonged to Matthew Browning; that was obvious.

She was no closer to her *place* than when she had left the Smokies, and she would have to leave Leesboro in the morning. Had she been mistaken about everything? She had been wrong before, but if wrong this time, then what? That old fear of being smothered by clouds of uncertainty and confusion was creeping back in. It crept in on cat paws so silently and so menacingly that it brought a chill as icy as the dark waters of the Oconaluftee. She could not, would not live in that devastating state again. She would return to North Carolina, to a way of life that she had been forced to accept, and make the best of it. There was no peace, no joy, no pleasure in it, but she could continue to exist until she was no longer able to care for herself; and then what difference would it make? She was good at pretending; she had often been told that. She'd just pretend to those around her to be jubilant, then formulate a plan. Only one or two would be discerning enough to know the truth.

Before Adele spoke, Elizabeth knew she was agonizing over what to say and how to say it. She had done everything she could to help Elizabeth, but it just had not come together, and it was no one's fault. It was disconcerting to both of them. They had set out with such high hopes—one to help and one to begin afresh and anew. They had each prayed about their own roles, and now the curtain was coming down, on a disappointing drama.

They commiserated together as they headed back toward town. If either of them could come up with anything else to pursue, they would do it together. Adele felt that somehow she had let Elizabeth down. As they parted at the parsonage, they embraced warmly and with tears. Neither could accept this as final, so they vowed to keep in touch.

Elizabeth exchanged only a few pleasantries with Carol and Bill, declined dinner, and went on in to ready her things for the journey that lay before her. She would leave early and perhaps even wander a bit on the return. Anyway, who knew where she was—or cared? Who knew what she was doing—or cared? Wouldn't the world just keep on turning if she decided to get off? *Of course it would* she thought, as she burst into tears. Someone else could make better use of the space she had been occupying and the air she had been breathing!

She quietly sobbed into the pillow until her eyes were nearly swollen shut, her head throbbing, pounding so that the entire room seemed to be vibrating. She wanted to scream from the top of one of these mountains. Scream until the leaves left the trees, scream until the grass in these fertile valleys felt her hot tears and drew back into the black earth beneath it. Scream until the cool mountain streams turned putrid with its own dead. Had she again been brought to the end of herself just to be humiliated by all the elements around her?

An eternity later, she composed enough herself to make it to the shower. Hot water, almost scalding, flowing over her began to subdue the monster inside her head—and inside her spirit. When she emerged and wrapped herself in the huge bath towel, she collapsed on the bed. She didn't know how long she had lain there, but when she arose to dress, it was dark outside, and all was quiet. Her head was still pounding, so she took some of the strong, prescription pain medicine, crawled into bed, and entered into a night of drug-induced, nightmare-riddled sleep.

Here to Help

Awakening to bright sunlight from what appeared to be a sun already high in the sky, Elizabeth turned to focus on the antique clock on the dresser. Eight forty-five! Eight forty-five? *My word,* she thought. *I was going to be miles from this place by this time. Carol and Preacher Bill probably think I have died in here.*

She jerked on her slippers and robe, raked a brush through her hair, splashed water on her swollen face, and hurried from the room. She could hear muffled voices coming from the kitchen as she made her way down the hall. As she was about to enter, she realized only one voice was speaking. It was Carol. She was standing at the door looking out toward the cemetery on the distant hill. She was praying. Tears were streaming down her face. She looked so young, so small, and so, so alone.

She must have sensed Elizabeth's presence, for she ended her prayer and tried to compose herself. Elizabeth, forgetting her own pain and problem, gathered the young woman in her arms as is a mother's way. She held her for a long time and then released her, asking what she could do to help.

Carol seated herself at the table where she had been studying earlier, her open Bible before her. Elizabeth made tea for both of them and sat down at the other end of the table and waited. She had learned long ago that quietly waiting was oftentimes the best, the only thing to do.

Setting her cup down carefully and deliberately, Carol picked up her Bible and began to speak.

"I've been searching here for hours for answers to hard question but I still haven't found them. All I keep getting is Psalm 46:10, 'Be still and know that I am God.' I've been brought back to that again and again."

Carol got up and walked slowly to the door. The glass in the storm door allowed her to look far off toward the surrounding mountains. Just beyond the cemetery, the national park began with rolling hills of grassland giving way to majestic mountains. There, wild honeysuckle and laurel nestled close to the trunks of towering cedars, hemlock, spruce, and beech and sweet gum.

"My mama went to be with the Lord just over a year ago; breast cancer. She went quickly, and as difficult as that was, I praise the Lord that she didn't linger and suffer."

She hesitated, and Elizabeth knew she was drawing on deep inner strength to continue. "She isn't buried there, of course, but when I really need to talk to her it just seems to help if I look toward the cemetery; maybe not to the cemetery so much as to the high places beyond. And I really needed her today. I don't know, somehow I just felt she could give me the words I could understand. I always looked to her for every answer, and I thought she could solve any problem. It still helps to talk to her."

"Is it something you could talk to me about?" Elizabeth knew she could be entering a place that was very private, one where perhaps she would not be welcome.

"I'm sure I do not have answers either, but I'm a good listener." Again she remembered other places and other days.

"I really don't want to burden you. I know you're dealing with not having had any luck with the property and all." She hesitated, but before Elizabeth could protest, she continued. "You remember the Jamisons from church, Doc and Anna Louise and Joe Bob?"

When Elizabeth nodded, she went on. "Well, they live on their grandparents' property just out of town about two miles. Their granddaddy passed away about a month ago, and they have just found out that he had a mortgage on the property and was behind in his payments. I think he borrowed money to pay for his wife's medical needs. Anyway, none of them knew any of that until Doc started to take care of everything after Mr. Jamison passed away. They're real proud people, so they haven't told anybody but Bill and me. The whole situation is real complicated, but they don't seem to have any way of holding on to their place, and they don't have anywhere else to go. Anna Louise called earlier and wanted me to come out and just be with her for a while, but Bill has gone to Roanoke to make hospital visits, and my car is in the shop; you know, from yesterday. She understood, but I'm really bothered that I can't be there for her."

Elizabeth's heart went out to both Carol and Anna Louise. Forgetting that she had a long journey ahead of her, she found herself saying, "Would it be okay, you think, if you and I went out to see her together? Do you think she would consider that an intrusion on my part?"

Carol's face brightened. "Oh, would you? I've told Anna Louise about you, and I think it would be fine, but I'll call and ask anyway. I know you need to get on the road, but …"—she wavered, tears welling—"it would be almost like she and I would each have our own mother there to help us through this hard place."

Elizabeth patted her hand and said, "Now you make that call, and I'll dress and throw my face on and we'll be off. I have no idea what to do or what to say, but we'll leave that up to the Lord." *And I'll just have to leave my trip up to the Lord, too,* she thought. *If I'm forced to travel in the dark, I'll just look to His light.*

As she quickly dressed, she thought about the headache pain of the night before and lifted up a prayer of thanksgiving for its absence. Strangely enough, she didn't have the horrible after-effects that customarily followed those bouts. She got ready in record time and rushed from the room, purse in hand, to find Carol beaming and reaching for the door.

"You'll have to direct me, Carol. Though I think I've covered every inch of ground in this part of the world, I haven't yet been to the Jamison's'."

"Oh, it's not far, but you wouldn't even know it was there if somebody didn't show you. Turn right just up ahead at Elm Street, then right again onto Park Road. Then I'll show you their road."

"Well, I haven't been this way. I can't believe it; it's as if we just spirited ourselves from town to the country and beautiful Parkway country at that. Look at those magnificent trees." Elizabeth was amazed at the beauty of the early autumn that opened up so quickly before them.

"There! There's the road," Carol said quickly. "See, you'd almost miss it. It doesn't look as if it goes anywhere, does it?"

Soon the old farmhouse came into view, and Elizabeth had to use every ounce of will power within her to keep from shouting. *That's it! That's the place I have been searching for. I knew I'd know it when I saw it!* She realized, though, that she couldn't say any of those things. This was not a piece of real estate on the market. This was the home of three beautiful people, and they were struggling to hold on to it. Carol had told her that the Jamison family had been one of the very earliest to settle in these parts and that much of the Park had once belonged to them.

If Elizabeth had been confused before, she was now even more so. She had been given a mental picture of her *home*, and this was it! She knew God did not play cruel jokes on people, so something was going on that she didn't yet understand. Maybe they were going to work something out and sell the property after all. But she knew she didn't have anywhere near enough to buy it even if that were the case. To try to figure out what was going on would be an exercise in futility. And she couldn't begin to use that much property, but what a shame it would be to break it up. To turn that paradise into a subdivision or shopping center would be blasphemous.

As Elizabeth started to pull up in front of the engaging old farmhouse Carol quickly directed her on past it to a smaller but equally lovely little cabin just down the drive. It looked like something out of a fairy tale—a simple little cottage nestled up against the protective forest. Elizabeth found herself just soaking up the beauty that lay before her. It looked as if a masterful fiber artist had woven a shawl of every color of the rainbow and gently laid it around the shoulders of the cabin, allowing only its smiling door to show. For days she had been enjoying the breathtaking beauty of God's creation, but nothing compared to this. It appeared that not one single leaf had been placed without painstaking care. The reds, yellows, oranges, browns, and greens— they had all been placed perfectly as had the varying shades of all of them. Only God could weave such an overwhelmingly beautiful tapestry. *I will try*, Elizabeth vowed silently, *to engrave this picture on my brain so that when gray days come upon me I can superimpose this over them. Oh, the majesty that is wrought by the hand of my Father.*

"The big house there is where the grandparents lived," Carol said, bringing Elizabeth out of her reverie. "It must be over a hundred years old, but isn't it beautiful? I've only been in it a time or two. It's just as wonderful inside—the kind of place that just invites you to curl up with a good book in one of the big easy chairs and never leave. Bill says it should be on the National Historical Registry. For some reason it just makes you think of home and family and a simpler, better way of life."

"It certainly is something," Elizabeth said. "It would be a shame for them to lose it."

"Oh, I know," Carol quickly responded, and Elizabeth could hear the pain in her voice. The heart of this precious young woman was breaking for her friends. Yes, she was showing the compassion that was hers to do in the role of a pastor's wife, but it was much more than that. Hers was such a sympathetic spirit that she would have displayed that same manner even if she hadn't been the pastor's wife. *Such a rare gift in this present world,* Elizabeth thought.

They stopped the car and hurried up the steps. Elizabeth could tell that this house and these grounds had been cared for by someone with great pride and diligence. Only those two attributes and hearts full of love turned out such work as had been done here.

"Please come in," Anna Louise said with such a cheerful voice that it almost took Elizabeth aback. "Ms. Barrington, I'm so glad you came, and I thank you for bringing my prayer partner to me." Only then could the pain be seen in her clear emerald eyes. "We always pray together from our respective places, but today I just needed a hug, too."

Anna Louise and Carol had already warmly embraced, and Elizabeth found her own arms and heart open to this young woman as naturally as could be.

"Thank you, Anna Louise, for allowing me to share this prayer time with you. I feel honored."

Elizabeth had dismissed her earlier thoughts about the property. This was not the time to be consumed with her needs and problems. This family needed answers from God, and if anyone knew what it felt like to have your home taken from you, she did.

Joe Bob had quietly entered the living room, where the ladies were now seated. On the coffee table lay a well-worn open Bible. Elizabeth could see that many passages had been highlighted, a practice she herself engaged in. Sadness filled her heart as she glanced at Joe Bob. He had the wide nose, the thick tongue, and the flattened forehead she had seen in so many with his type of genetic makeup. His arms and legs appeared too short for his body. As he waited courteously until his sister invited him into the conversation, she couldn't help feeling that God had endowed him with some special gifts that far outweighed his limitations.

"Sister, may I serve you and your guests some tea? I've already fixed a tray." He spoke with such grace and pride Elizabeth felt that she was in the presence of an angel.

"Yes, thank you, Joe Bob, but first let me introduce you to Ms. Barrington. She is going to come here to live in our community," she stated in such a way that it was as if it had already happened. He stepped across the room and extended his little hand.

"Hello, Ms. Barrington. You worshiped with us on Wednesday night. I saw you there. I'm glad you're coming here to live. Then you can worship with us all the time, and you can come with Miss Carol to visit, and I can serve you tea."

He smiled and excused himself to go and bring in the tea. He was very careful as he first set the heavy silver tray on a side table and then handed each of them a delicate, embroidered linen napkin. He then lifted the beautiful, ornate china cups as if he were touching the most precious gifts on earth. He placed the silver infuser carefully over each cup, poured the steaming tea, and replaced the pot back on the tray. After serving each of them, he replaced the cozy on the pot and offered sugar, lemon, or cream. Next came the delicate tea cakes, which he gently placed on plates with tongs. He waited in front of each lady for her to accept or decline and then moved on. He was so adept at his job one could think he had been schooled in the art of tea serving in London, no less. Pleased with a job well done, he again excused himself with a big smile, quietly telling his sister he would be on the porch listening to his CD if she needed him.

Elizabeth had, before arriving, felt that she might have been intruding, but as Anna Louise began to pour out her heart to them she knew that was not the case. Only after Mr. Jamison had passed away had she and her brothers been made aware of the financial burden he had been carrying. His wife's medical needs had been so great that he had borrowed money from some unscrupulous people, not realizing that he had signed a mortgage that he would never be able to pay back. He had even let his taxes go unpaid. Thinking he was protecting his grandchildren from worry, he had not discussed any of this with them. A letter had just come demanding payment in full by Monday or foreclosure proceedings would begin. Also, the county was demanding payment of the taxes. The lien on the property was not a huge amount of money, but it was more than they could come up with. Knowing the value of the land, the lien holders weren't willing to work out any arrangements. They were simply going to seize the property—by the close of business on Monday.

"This is our home," Anna Louise said through tears. "We have nothing but this place. Only God knows how to deal with this situation. I know He'll take care of us, but I'm just so concerned about Doc and Joe Bob. I don't think Doc can handle much more. He's only recently begun to heal."

She continued on, sometimes with uncontrollable weeping, emptying her soul before them. Elizabeth, sitting quietly, learned that this little family had been through more pain and suffering than the writer of any novel could begin to imagine. The cruel twists and turns that fate had dealt them and that they had been forced to endure day after day were simply unbelievable. Before one tragedy had ended another had begun. And just when they were feeling somewhat settled, another difficulty had arisen. As she tried to absorb it all, Elizabeth could hear the words of a dear preacher friend.

"Sister," he had said, "God only allows real testing in the lives of those He can trust it to, and then He brings them out of it as fine gold, tried in the fire." Surely this family was gold of the purest kind, in its most refined form.

Elizabeth felt sure that Carol already knew most of what Anna Louise was saying, but she was just allowing her the space to pour the pain out of her soul. Strange how cleansing and healing that simple act can be. Even in the midst of all the pain, there was not one hint of bitterness toward anyone. Truly, here was evidence in the flesh of God's sustaining grace and the truth of the existence of the wonderful Holy Spirit and His indwelling. Only through His power could she and her brothers have survived and remained absolutely faithful.

The Jamisons

Anna Louise had married her high school sweetheart, John David Wilkes, just two months after her graduation. J. D., as he was called, was two years older than she and was already in Officer Candidate School. He had known all his life that he wanted to be a Navy Seal. They married while he was home on furlough and left immediately for his final months of training.

Both her family and his went down for his graduation. "Not only was he in the top of his class," Anna Louise had said with all the love and pride of her heart spilling forth, "he was the most handsome, too!" He came home for a short leave, then shipped out to places unknown aboard the USS *Abraham Lincoln*.

Twenty days later he, along with two of his ship mates, was killed in a freak diving accident. It was to have been a normal exercise. What had gone wrong? Everyone believed their gear had been tampered with, but it couldn't be officially proven, so it went on the record as "a tragic, yet unavoidable accident."

By her own testimony, only faith in God and the ministering hands of His children brought Anna Louise through the tragedy. "My family and my church carried me," she would say. Every time she played the beautiful song, "God Makes No Mistakes" the entire church wept and worshiped.

Two years later, Clint and Pauline Jamison were killed just eight miles from home in a car crash. They were returning from Washington, DC, where Clint had spoken to a Senate subcommittee concerning the preservation of wilderness in their area. The driver of an eighteen wheeler had fallen asleep at the wheel, crossed into their lane, and hit them head on. They, as well as the driver, were killed instantly. Demonstrating the genuine grace and love of God, the entire community reached out to the family. In turn, Doc, Anna Louise, and Joe Bob extended Christian love and compassion to the young widow and children of the trucker. In so doing, they were able to win her to the Lord and brought all of them into the fellowship of the church.

Anna Louise turned the energy of her emotions of grief into hands of help. For quite some time she helped care for the children while the widowed mother prepared to reenter the work force. As is God's way, a position became available at the hospital for which she was well qualified and where she would have child care on site.

The grandparents, Clint's folks, were wonderful, godly people who loved their only grandchildren unconditionally. They helped out in every way they could, but they were limited when it came to finances. Doc had just begun medical school at Duke University in North Carolina but could not relieve himself of the heavy weight of responsibility for his younger sister and brother, so he soon dropped out. He was able to complete enough work to become a Physician's Assistant. His plan was to join the medical team at the local hospital. However, Dr. Robb, the only veterinarian in the area, persuaded him to come work at the clinic.

Clinton Joseph Jamison III had been called Doc for as long as any of his friends could remember. From the time he was a kid, he had attended to any and all medical needs that anyone would allow. It was quite an ordinary sight to see some local kid with a splint on his arm or a bandage on his head—though they had been no injury at all. And of course, he was often found at the EMS office or Dr. Robb's clinic. Thus, he seemed to be content using his skills at the clinic. Everybody around had complete confidence in him, and most would have been as secure in having him as their doctor as they were in his being their vet.

Like so many good ol' boys, Doc seemed to be following the same path that others in Leesboro were on. He had a home, lots of friends, a position at the church and in the community, and a girl that everybody just assumed would become his wife one day. Doc must have thought that, too, for he was making plans to build a house on his grandparents' farm.

Doc and Donna had been best friends since grade school. Somewhere around junior high, their relationship began to evolve into more than just friends. By the time they graduated high school, everybody expected to be hearing an announcement. When Doc went off to college at the University of Virginia, Donna went too. She had always loved art and decided to major in graphic design. She was very gifted, and soon many doors of opportunity began to open for her. She was traveling to New York, Atlanta, and Los Angeles. Still, she and Doc were the inseparable pair, whenever possible. They both graduated college the same year and started making serious plans about their life together. When Doc left for Duke, Donna left for a job with a big advertising agency in Atlanta, still with her plans to go wherever necessary as a doctor's wife. When Doc had to drop out of medical school, Donna saw that she was not going to be living the "country club" life that she had envisioned. It was then that she began to put distance between herself and Doc. She was making a real name for herself in the corporate world, jet setting all over the continent, and spending more and more time in New York and Los Angeles, Paris, Rome, and Hong Kong. The last time anyone saw her was when she came home to move her widowed mother to "a little place I've bought for her just outside Atlanta."

Here, in the heart of the Shenandoah Valley, in the shadow of the Alleghenies and the Blue Ridge Mountains, life continues on. Resilient mountain folk adapt to the changes and accept the new paths that have been laid out before them. So it was with the Jamisons. Doc stayed busy at the clinic, led the choir at church, and otherwise played his music, sang his songs, and continued to be the rock for the rest of the family. Grandma and Grandpa, now up in years, found themselves leaning more and more on their grandchildren. They had always been the family's leaders, but now it was time to hand over the reins.

When Grandma became ill, Anna Louise stepped in and took over her household duties, thus keeping one house for her and her brothers and one for her grandparents. She had to walk a fine line between helping out and not making Grandpa feel that he was not needed. Joe Bob was wonderful with the outside work and did everything well and with a joyful heart. All the local folk remarked about their gardens being showplaces.

Less than six months after Grandma's passing, Grandpa went to join her. Their losses were shared by the entire community, but instead of sadness there was a time of celebration at both funerals. Two precious saints had gone home and were now receiving their rewards for lives lived in obedience to their Savior. Their places on the pews were empty, but deep, loving memories permeated the entire building as a sweet-smelling savor, wafting up and down every aisle.

Life for the Jamisons was not sad. They just lived their lives in reality and truth. Always, they gave God glory for His goodness and accepted each trial and tragedy with dignity and grace. They, each of them, had learned that the time on this side of eternity was only a whisper or a vapor as compared to what lay ahead. One day they, too, would receive their rewards, and they were always busy laying up treasures in heaven. Their desires individually and collectively were to be good, strong, and ready soldiers of the cross. The town of Leesboro was a better place because of them.

Bewildered, Elizabeth listened as the two young women discussed the bleak situation. She kept trying to figure out the real reason she was here. Yes, Carol had needed a ride, but was there something more? Something she was supposed to be doing or at least learning? Maybe, as Carol had said, she was just to be a motherly presence; if so, she could certainly do that. She could hold and comfort and commiserate with these two girls. She had been in that position many times before.

They almost unconsciously knelt and begun to call out quietly to the Lord for this present need. None of them had given any thought to how much time they had spent there until the sound of a vehicle interrupted their prayers. Anna Louise rose swiftly and went to the door. It was Doc with the preacher close behind. They rushed in, both talking at the same time. Elizabeth wasn't sure if they were excited or agitated, but they definitely had something to say. She started to excuse herself and go out to the porch, but both men stopped her. The women exchanged amazed looks and took their seats.

No sooner had they seated themselves than Adele came running into the room with a tall, distinguished gentleman not far behind. It was evident that Anna Louise, Carol, and Elizabeth were the only ones not privy to what was going on. Whatever it was, it must have been of great concern to them. The room fell silent. Who was going to explain?

Preacher Bill went to the center of the room.

"Uh, folks. Uh, I'm sure we all have the same subject on our minds right now. And I'm sure every single one of us has been in prayer concerning the problem. I know that's what I was doing all the way back from Roanoke. When I pulled in at the church I found Doc sitting on the steps. He has some interesting questions and even more interesting ideas. After much discussion, we decided we needed some legal advice. That's where Denton came in."

He turned to Doc who took up the conversation. "After Denton answered my most immediate questions, I tried to find you, Ms. Barrington."

"But he got me instead," Adele jumped in. "I sure hope you don't mind us talking 'bout you behind your back."

If Elizabeth had been bewildered before, she was now dumbfounded.

"I don't understand," she said, looking from one to another. She knew Adele's husband's name was Denton and that he was a lawyer, but they had never formally met. What in the world did he have to do with her?

"Let me try to explain, Ms. Barrington," Doc continued. Now Carol and Anna Louise too were waiting expectantly, staring wide-eyed at Doc and the preacher.

"All of us here know that you have been looking for property," Doc said as he sat down on the sofa near Elizabeth. "Adele told us what you wanted to do."

Adele looked toward Elizabeth, hoping she had not spoken out of turn. Elizabeth smiled and nodded at Adele. She had made no secret of her intentions. Adele breathed a sigh of relief and started to speak, but Doc continued.

"Well, there might be a way we could help each other—probably mostly me, if you'd care to hear."

The excitement in the room would have gone out the top of the Richter scale.

"Please go on!" Elizabeth almost screamed. "We all want to hear what you are talking about." She unconsciously had placed herself in the group as one of *them*. All the women nodded and thought nothing of her self-inclusion. She had been accepted into their fold from the very beginning.

Doc started, "Maybe I should just ask some questions first. Your answers might stop this whole wild hair notion at square one."

Elizabeth nodded expectantly. He went on. "Okay. First how do you like what you've seen of the Jamison place so far? Could it possibly fit your need?"

She could hardly find her voice. "Oh, my word! This place is lovely … it's more than lovely … it's … it's … wonderful. It would more than fit my need … but there's no way …"

Doc interrupted, "Hear me out … all of you." He had observed the shocked looks on the faces of his sister and Carol. "You know how much money we must come up with by Monday if we are to save our home. And Ms. Barrington, Adele told us what price range property you were looking for. After conferring with Denton, we think we might be able to strike a business deal. Denton says if you are interested, you could, in a very legitimate way, buy our property for just what we owe, and then you could assign us a one hundred year lease to allow us to live on the property. We would live here in our cabin, and you could assume ownership of the big house and everything else. There are over two hundred acres, you know. You could do whatever you want. We would know that it was really yours. Denton can explain all the legality of this idea, if you think you would want to consider the plan."

Again the room fell silent. Elizabeth's head was spinning. Every eye was filled with tears. Anna Louise, with her hand over her mouth to hold in sobs, excused herself to put on tea and coffee.

Elizabeth didn't trust her own voice. She felt sure if she tried to speak she would awaken from this unbelievable dream. Not knowing whether she could or not, she tried standing. Her legs felt like wet noodles. She moved slowly and quietly toward the door. It felt as if it weighed a ton as she pushed it open. Breathing deeply, she allowed the fresh country air to fill her lungs, removing the cobwebs that had taken over her brain. When she was sure she could think clearly and not faint, she reentered the room. All eyes were on her.

She began to speak softly as she sat down.

"I … I hardly know what to say; what questions to ask first. Did I hear correctly? Doc? Mr. Curry? Please forgive me for being so slow, but I need you to start at the very beginning and explain all this to me."

"Of course," Doc said. "If I didn't know God had spoken to me about this, I would be sure that I had lost my mind."

"Ms. Barrington," Denton Curry began. "This is not an everyday kind of action, but it's not totally unheard of either. Mostly though, I will say it usually occurs among family members. Let me jump ahead—the one hundred year lease deal could have a stipulation attached that would extend it for one hundred more years; and on and on. Now back to the beginning. Doc purposed that you buy from him and his siblings the entire Jamison farm for just what is being demanded of them by both the tax office and the lien holders. The deed would be transferred to you at that moment, just as would happen for any other piece of property you would buy outright. The only difference would be the lease. He also would like to ask you to give them first opportunity to purchase the property back from you if you ever decide to sell. Of course, it is all completely legal, and I would welcome you having your own attorney discuss everything and look over all the papers before you signed anything."

As Elizabeth began to speak it seemed that her words were coming from somewhere deep within her; words that she hadn't even formed.

"This is Friday, and it will soon be noon. There are so many questions that must be answered. First, I need to get my attorneys on the phone. Mr. Curry, you will need to fax or e-mail to them everything you have told me. I'll give you their number. Then I'll need to look at the house and at least some of the property. All of that will need to be done in time for me to be able to make bank transfers that could be in place by Monday. Thank God for modern technology. Let's go up to the house; you too, Doc. I'll make the call and we'll go from there."

Of the few business deals Elizabeth had made, she had never made one so quickly. Anything of such great importance required much prayer, thought, and planning. However, her heart, soul, mind, and spirit were at peace. Much prayer, thought, and planning had *already* been done. Had not they, like Peter's friends, been in prayer when the answer presented itself at the door undeniably and in person? In this case, two answers had come in one. Now, only the logistics were not completely clear. She smiled confidently, rose from her seat, and stood on firm, strong legs. She reached for her telephone and headed for the door. Denton, Adele, and Doc followed—a willing entourage. Carol, Anna Louise, Joe Bob and the preacher stayed behind "to make sandwiches for lunch whenever you're ready."

As they went slowly up the drive, Elizabeth observed everything with a much more discerning eye than when she and Carol had come down it earlier. By the time they reached the farm house, she had gotten Franklin on the phone. He assured her that he and Kendra would be there in time to join her for brunch tomorrow. Though she would never have asked them to come, she was so glad they would be there to explain anything she might not understand. Denton and Adele left her and Doc to go through the house. They would go back to town to begin drawing up the papers, so everything would be in order if she decided to make the deal. Feeling understandably apprehensive but amazingly excited, she followed Doc up the cobblestone path to the wide front steps and the big porch with its oak rockers and old country swing.

Doc took a deep breath as if he thought going through the farm house door was going to require a lot of intestinal fortitude. The truth was that this old house held a lifetime of memories—many happy but also many sad. Now that his grandparents were gone, it was very difficult for him to enter. He still always expected to be greeted by one of them; more likely Grandma wiping her hands on her apron and inviting him into the kitchen for a glass of tea or a slice of freshly baked bread. This house had once held so much love and so much laughter. Even when life brought disappointments and difficulties, just coming here helped lessen the pain. It had been quite some time since it rang with joy, but he knew the walls could still tell the stories that would be comforting. He hadn't even given thought as to what to do with it since Grandpa's death, especially with the weight of the lien hanging over him. Was it now time to step back and view the whole picture from outside the pain? Was that even possible? Was he just grasping at straws?

His sister and brother were his responsibility, but he had finally turned them and the whole situation over to God. After that surrender, he had gone to the church to speak with his pastor. That's when the pastor found him sitting on the steps, waiting. He would follow God's leadership, whatever that was. He knew he could trust His hand and would understand His leading.

Just before reaching the door, Doc turned and spoke in a voice so low it was almost a whisper. "We ... we haven't gone through their things yet. Everything is just the way it was when ..." He turned back and gently turned the big glass door knob. Elizabeth noticed that it was not even locked.

"I don't think a single day goes by that Anna Louise and Joe Bob don't come up here. Joe Bob knows Grandma and Grandpa are in heaven, but he seems to be so happy in this house. He continues to sweep the porches, water the plants, and weed the flower gardens, just as he has always done."

Perfect!

Elizabeth wasn't sure what she expected to find, but when Doc held the door open for her to enter, her heart skipped a beat. She was instantly transported back in time, back to a more beautiful, more genteel time. She half expected to be ushered into the spacious parlor by a maid, offered tea and scones, and told to make herself comfortable until the lady of the house came down. She was glad Doc was moving slowly, for she wanted to indelibly print this picture in her mind. The glistening wood floors, the grandfather clock, and the open Bible on the library table captivated her. The reason for her being here was unimportant at that moment. Just being here was paramount. She quietly followed Doc, barely hearing him as they moved from room to room.

He was telling her the history of the house and the family. She knew these things were important, but not right now. She felt as if she were intruding and should apologize for looking and touching. This house was a museum, a living testimony and memorial to the lives of those who had gone before.

She had been in farm houses before and always loved the huge rooms with their high ceilings, polished floors, and tall windows. Most of the ones she had visited though had suffered from lack of care over the years. Not this one! She, too, almost expected Grandma Jamison to come out of the kitchen to give them each a big motherly hug. This place even smelled good, not at all what she expected. There was no dust, mustiness, or unpleasant odor anywhere. She felt sure that was due to the meticulous care of Anna Louise and Joe Bob.

Without any explanation, she could see that the bedroom with its tiny cot in the corner had at one time been the master bedroom. The absence of the double bed told her that it had been replaced for a time by a hospital bed. In this room a loving husband had cared for the love of his life in her declining years, catching a wink or two on the little cot when he could. She was sure he only allowed the hospice workers to help in areas that he was unable to. She blinked back tears and quickly followed Doc out of the room.

She noticed that as they ascended the stairs there was one step—only one—that squeaked. She could see a teenager coming in late who had learned to step high over it, hoping to avoid disturbing a napping parent. And she smiled as she saw that same burly kid bounding down the next morning, not minding the noise at all.

Now on the landing, Elizabeth found herself bathed in brilliant sunlight. The roof of the spacious porch below had arrested the rays, but here they came pouring in unhindered, warming both body and soul. She couldn't resist the window seat with its cushions and handmade crazy quilt. Leaning up against the warm glass she could see the turrets on either side. She knew without looking that there were two bedrooms, each one boasting a window seat as well, where books were read, where stories of princes and princesses were written and dragons were slain.

The one on the right had a fireplace with a hand-carved chestnut mantle and a brass fan screen just like the ones she had seen earlier in the parlor and master bedroom. Three identical iron beds stood resolutely waiting to bring rest and sweet dreams to tired little bodies. Covered with white chenille spreads and piled high with feather pillows, they could draw in the most rambunctious child. The big rocking chair was for the storyteller. Here, he would sit and spin yarns and tell tall tales until every little head nodded and every little eye closed. Then with a kiss on every brow, he tucked the warm quilts under every chin and tiptoed quietly out, only to return before he extinguished the house lights, just to make sure all was well.

Doc was moving more quickly now from room to room. Sensing the pain in his soul, Elizabeth willed herself not to linger. Perhaps, she would ask if she might come back alone tomorrow. Then she would take hours to wander through. She wanted to absorb every detail, commit every image to memory.

Here, on the second floor were four bedrooms and two bathrooms. With the big master suite downstairs, she knew this house could accommodate lots of guests. Had she drawn a house plan and outlined every desired detail, she could not have come any closer to what was here. Was this for real? Never in her wildest dreams or most fervent prayers had she thought something like this possible. She must not get overly excited; it was not a done deal yet. What was God's complete plan? Surely there was much she couldn't yet see or understand. Would He allow her to know more right now, or was she just to continue to rest in His arms as He continued to care for her? She smiled. She had learned long ago that some things were to be kept and pondered in the heart.

As they started down the back stairs, Joe Bob came running toward the house, panting hard and yelling for Doc at the top of his lungs. Doc hurried down and caught him as he burst in the back door.

"What's wrong, son? Slow down before you pass out."

"Doc, Doc! Sister says you got to call Dr. Robb right now. Somethin's wrong with somebody's horse. You got to hurry."

"Okay, okay. Just calm down. I'll be right there."

As he turned to look at Elizabeth, she quickly spoke. "It's fine, Doc. Maybe I can come back tomorrow if that's okay with you."

"Sure, that'll be fine."

Just then Preacher Bill pulled up at the back door. "Thought I'd come get y'all. The girls got sandwiches ready down at the house, and you do need to call Dr. Robb, Doc."

Joe Bob had collapsed on the back steps, stretching out on the porch. Seeing Elizabeth he looked embarrassed and jumped up immediately. He brushed himself off, removed his cap, and dropped his head.

"I'm fine, Ms. Liz-beth. Guess I just ran too fast."

"I believe you did. But I'm glad you're fine. Come on with me. Let's go see if we can get you a big glass of your sister's delicious iced tea."

"Yes, ma'am. That'll be good. That'll fix me right up. And a sandwich, too. Sister makes good sandwiches."

He took her hand and gently led her down the steps. He ran ahead and opened the truck door, waited for her to get in, and closed it firmly behind her. Smiling that angelic smile of his, he climbed onto the back, leaned on the side with his arms folded under his chin, and settled in to wait for Doc and the preacher.

Preacher Bill bounded over the side and sat down the same way Joe Bob had. No wonder these people loved their pastor so much. He truly was a man for all seasons, a man for all people. He was as much at home as a boy in a pickup truck as he was a comforter, a counselor, a deliverer of the gospel. How quickly had he and the rest of these people taken up residence in her heart. They had moved in to stay—lock, stock, and barrel.

"Oh, dear me, not dessert, too."

Anna Louise smiled and placed the fresh apple pie a la mode in front of Elizabeth. "The apples are from that knotty, gnarled up tree at the edge of my backyard. It's so pitiful looking! I look at it every winter and think, *You'll never make it through this one,* but every spring it's the first one to burst forth with buds. And it always bears so many apples I can't begin to use them all. I'm not even sure what kind of apple it is."

Joe Bob interrupted his sister, "I know what it is, Sister. It's the best apple pie apple! That's what it is. Grandma told me so!"

"I think you're right, Joe Bob", Elizabeth smiled and patted his arm. "Maybe you should name it *Grandma's Apple Pie Tree.* What do you think?"

"I think that's a good name. Don't you, Sister?"

"Yes, I do." Anna Louise was about to say something more but was interrupted by the ringing of a telephone.

"Oh, my," Elizabeth said with a start. "I think that is my phone. Who'd be calling me here?"

She retrieved it from her purse and recognizing the caller answered it with a questioning, "Hello? Yes. Is something wrong? Uh, just a minute." Turning to the others at the table she said, "Will you excuse me for a moment? Yes, yes, Kendra, I'm here." She quickly walked through the house and out onto the porch, all the while listening intently.

"I see. Yes, of course. I can do that. You had me scared to death. I thought surely something was wrong. Now, let me get a pen, so I can make a note of everything I need to get. Just a minute."

Retrieving a note pad and pen from her purse, she sat poised in the porch swing. With more confidence than before she said to Kendra, "Okay! Shoot!"

Kendra laughed, picturing her dear friend sitting all prim and proper, tiny phone wedged between her shoulder and ear, pen hovering over her signature blue-flowered note pad ready to take down every detailed instruction.

"He wants you to go to the hall of records; I don't know if it will be at the courthouse or if they have a city hall, but anyway, here's what you'll need to get copies of: the deed to the property, the tax bill for last year, and maybe the last evaluation, too, also a plat of the property. If there has been a recent survey, you should get a copy of that, too.

"Hopefully these will show clearly all the boundaries and the exact acreage, etc. With the deed, there should be registered any and all liens and any other binding contracts against the property. If those vulturious people did not register their contracted deal with the grandfather, it isn't legal anyway. But even if they didn't, if his verifiable signature is on a mortgage or deed of trust that they hold, we'll still have to handle it through the court.

"Those are the most significant pieces of paper that we will need, initially anyway. Franklin and I can go over them tomorrow and prepare our strategy. Then, FYI, while you're there you may want to get a copy of their zoning laws. Might as well know exactly what we're doing before we do it, huh?"

"Okay. I'll do my best. I'm no paralegal, you know." They both laughed at the private joke.

"I know you're not, but you'll only be doing the same thing you helped me with on that trip to Louisville. Remember?"

"Oh, I do remember. I can do this. Piece of cake! Kendra, on a more serious note, I can't begin to tell you how much I appreciate your coming up here and all. You and Franklin are the best!"

"Of course we are," Kendra quickly replied in her lighthearted manner. "Seriously, Liddy, we would have it no other way. You know how much you mean to us. At least now we know where you are and what you are up to! And anyway we need a few days away from the office. This trip will be for us as much as for you. You take care. Call me if you need me. We'll get some breakfast on the road and be there in time to do some brainstorming before lunch." Elizabeth tarried only a few more minutes, then returned to the dining room, where the others were just finishing up.

"I'm so sorry. I didn't mean to be so rude, especially after you fed me so well. Anna Louise, you must give me your chicken salad recipe, and the apple pie one, too. I've never had better, of either."

Anna Louise blushed and continued stacking plates. "I saved you another piece of pie. The ice cream melted on the first one, so Joe Bob took it out to the puppies."

"Oh, my goodness! Even the puppies eat like kings around here. Well, that's the last time they're getting my dessert."

Elizabeth tousled Joe Bob's hair and told them that the call was from her friend back home. Kendra had suggested that she do the paper search alone. *You never can tell,* she had said. That troubled Elizabeth somewhat, but she chose not to dwell on it. *Don't borrow trouble; it will find you soon enough!* Sage advice from days gone by.

"My attorney wants me to do some things for him in town. And I need to see about getting him and his wife a place to stay for a couple of nights."

Both Anna Louise and Carol were quick to offer accommodations, but Elizabeth politely declined. She knew it might be necessary for her and Franklin and Kendra to talk privately. There was so much to discuss and so many questions yet to be answered. If she were going to make life decisions in one weekend, she must leave no stone unturned.

She thanked Anna Louise again for the delicious lunch and more importantly for the sweet fellowship. After making sure Preacher Bill would be able to take Carol to pick up her car, she said her good-byes. She stopped just before reaching the door. "Carol," she said, as if terribly embarrassed. "I … I … haven't even asked if I might stay with you a few more days. I'm acting as if I live at your house. I'm sure I could get a room in town."

Carol and Bill both laughed and reached out to grasp her hands. Bill spoke very authoritatively. "Nonsense. You know you can stay as long as you want. We like you *living* with us. We would be devastated if you went to a motel. It'd be like turning my own mother out. We'll see you at *home* when you've finished your business in town."

The subject was closed. They followed her out and waved until she was out of sight. Elizabeth entered into an attitude of prayer as she drove away, and this time she was much more concerned about others than herself.

Oh, thank You, God, for these beautiful people. And please God, do something spectacular in their lives. Help me in some way to be for them what they have so graciously been for me. Surely You have some plan that includes all of us—somehow together. Help me to be sensitive to Your leadership and not miss one opportunity to be an instrument in Your hand to touch their lives for good. It brings such joy to see young people who exhibit the gift of the Spirit in such marvelous ways. I've already seen, too, the gifts and talents that You have bestowed on each of them. Oh, God! You have brought me here. I don't know if it's only for a day or a lifetime, but I will never forget this day. I have seen Your face.

Strange Happenings

Not knowing how long it might take for her to secure all the requested documents, Elizabeth headed straight for the courthouse. It was an impressive old building with enormous stone columns and wide steps. She loved the big caps on the steps and could imagine children sitting there while their daddies talked business with the town leaders.

Inside, her heels made clacking sounds on the polished marble floor that reverberated throughout the long hallway. Finding an information slate on the left wall, she was able to see that all the offices she needed to visit were indeed in this building; just another attribute of a small town. As she started toward the elevator, her eyes were drawn upward to the second-floor landing. Stepping back several steps, she could clearly see that the Ten Commandments had been beautifully chiseled into the wall along the landing. Making a mental note to come back with her camera, she hurried into the elevator.

Coming off on the third floor, she saw the tax office directly in front of her. *Might as well start here,* she thought. Inside, she was greeted by a pleasant, talkative young woman named Edie. She took a quick look at her notes and then explained what papers she needed.

"Sure, ma'am. Those are all public records. So, no problem at all. Come this way."

Elizabeth thanked her and started to make small talk when Edie stopped and turned. "You know, you're the second person this week to ask for those Jamison statements. Somethin' goin' on here that I should know about? I usually know 'bout everythin' that goes on round here." She laughed and patted Elizabeth on the arm. *I bet that's true,* thought Elizabeth. *Must have been Doc or Denton. Or was it?*

"I didn't know them guys, but they sure were sharp dressers and they were from Ad-lanna. I'd put money on that. I snuck a look at their car when they was leavin'. Big old Caddie with a Georgie license tag. Yep, they're big money men from down Hot-Lanna. You can bet on it!"

A chill ran over Elizabeth as from an Arctic wind. She shivered. If Edie were right, why were those *big money men from Atlanta* looking for tax information on the Jamison property? Was there something she should know?

"Didn't really want to give them the papers, but I didn't have no choice. Couldn't very well lie and say I couldn't find 'em, could I? I had to give 'em to 'em, just like I did for you. Oh, I didn't mind givin' 'em to you! You seem like a real nice lady, real nice indeed."

"Thank you, Edie." Elizabeth spoke in a calm, confident manner. "I'm sure there is nothing to be concerned about. They probably just made a mistake about the particular property. There are lots of pieces on the market, you know."

"You know, I bet you're right. Now why didn't I think of that. Oh, well, that's just me. I let this wild, *bored* imagination run away with me. Gotta stop doin' that. My boyfriend says I turn every simple request for information into a soap opera. But it keeps me from goin' crazy with paper shuffling."

Elizabeth smiled and excused herself as Edie, still talking, followed her all the way to the door. Elizabeth wondered if she were going to continue with her to her next destination, but she finally, reluctantly turned back to her *boring paper shuffling*.

Once back in the hall alone, Elizabeth took a minute to gather her thoughts. She need not waste energy trying to dissect that disturbing information. Probably meant nothing at all and especially not to her. She must keep her focus on the business at hand. Shaking her head as if to dispel the unpleasant thoughts, she walked on down to the office of the Register of Deeds. She was very glad she had brought along her old leather briefcase. She hadn't had a need for it in years, but for some reason she had thrown it in the car. Without it now she probably would have strewn papers all over the building.

Again referring to her notes, she was sure she had gotten copies of everything she needed. Most of them were written in legalese so she chose to deposit them in the briefcase until Franklin and Kendra were there to explain them to her. She wasn't even sure why they were so important, but she had enough confidence in her friends to do as they asked.

Next, she drove to the little motel she had seen as she came in. When they had passed it on Wednesday, Adele had told her that it was a clean, quiet family business that had been passed down from father to son. She hoped Adele was right, since it was the only lodging place within an hour's drive of Leesboro in any direction.

It was a neat little place called The Cozy Corner. A young, pregnant black woman greeted her with an outstretched hand. She did have one king room she said, down at the end of the row.

"We don't have but seven rooms and oddly enough we only have two empty right now; that king one and one with two doubles. It's unusual for us to fill up at this time of year. There's a nice group of business folk from Atlanta that are going to be here for several days, and they have taken several of the other rooms. Nice enough folk I guess, but I've hardly seen them since they checked in three days ago."

Business folk from Atlanta. Hum, Edie had been right! Elizabeth was visibly shaken. The young woman asked if she was okay. Embarrassed, she gave the explanation that her blood sugar had probably bottomed out. She'd go get some orange juice or something and she would be fine.

"I'll get you some. Here, sit down, and I'll be right back."

She went quickly through the door behind the counter and returned with a tall, chilled glass of juice. Elizabeth sipped it slowly and brought her emotions under control. Smiling weakly she told the young woman she would like to take a look at the room.

"Sure, I'll walk down there with you." She pulled a key from under the counter and held the door open for Elizabeth.

"Please excuse me for my ill manners. My name is Janice. My husband, Hildred, and I are the owners, operators, maids, maintenance people, and office managers of The Cozy Corner." She laughed; holding her protruding tummy as she slowly waddled down the narrow walk. "So if you have anything to report, good or bad; we're that department, too."

She unlocked the door and flipped on the light. Elizabeth followed her into the charming, tidy room. It was more spacious than she expected and very tastefully decorated; not at all an ordinary motel room.

"This is lovely, Janice. Did you do the decorating yourself?"

"Thank you, ma'am, and yes, I did. I don't mind telling you I would love to have been an interior decorator like my friend Mary Lynn. But Hilly's parents needed us to take over this little place, and we're perfectly happy here. I can still do my thing with paint and fabric and help my Hilly take care of his parents as well. I know it doesn't sound very exciting, and it certainly isn't glamorous, but we love it. We meet the nicest people, and we are together. His parents are still able to relieve us occasionally, so we're not totally tied down." She patted her tummy and smiled. "And just think how blessed our little one will be to be surrounded every day by all those who love him. I don't think anything is as important as that."

They chatted as if they were old friends as they walked back to the office. Elizabeth secured the room and told Janice she would bring the Laythons by as soon as they arrived tomorrow. Thanking her again, Elizabeth started back to her car. Parked next to her was a big, black Cadillac Escalade. *That wasn't there earlier; as a matter of fact, neither was that little sports car.* Intuitively, she stepped back to view the license plates. They were both from Georgia. *Just those business folk that Janice had mentioned,* she thought.

As she was about to back out, another car drove up. Hadn't she seen that very car somewhere before? And the pretty girl getting out, she knew her from somewhere, too. But where? The girl looked around suspiciously before donning a large, floppy hat and dark glasses, then hurried toward one of the rooms. She tapped lightly on the door two times, hesitated before knocking again. It opened just enough to allow her to slip inside. How strange! What would be going on in this quiet little town that would require such melodramatic secrecy? Feeling very uncomfortable, Elizabeth left the motel without looking back. *I don't usually let my imagination get the better of me, but this day is getting curiouser and curiouser!*

Driving back into town, Elizabeth kept trying to place the girl and her car. She finally dismissed it as her mind playing tricks on her. What business was it of hers if a dozen pretty girls were entering motel rooms? She had probably overdramatized the entire incident. Just someone going into a room, that's all it had been.

Since she was now going to be staying a few extra days, she knew she needed to pick up some personal items. She had seen an old-fashioned Five and Dime just down the street from the courthouse. It had a green and red, roll-up canvas awning and a bench out front. She could see in the window display the wooden barrels that had once held hard candy and the like. One of them had been turned upside down and now held a big checkerboard. On either side were two straight-backed wooden chairs. Even if she hadn't needed anything, she would have been drawn inside. The proprietor made her think of Michael, the manager of the hardware store back home. Strange how every small town has some of the exact same characters. Striking up a friendly conversation with him, she asked if Leesboro had a Better Business Bureau or a merchant's association. Michael told her the closest thing they had was the chamber of commerce.

"Mary Beth or Nancy can tell you almost anything you want to know about the town, and probably a lot that you don't want to know," he said with a hearty laugh. "They'll be there 'til five, and a lot longer if you get them wound up."

She checked her watch—four forty-five, just enough time to get a few answers. She really did need to know something about special tourist attractions, any seasonal events of significance, volume of traffic through town, etc. The only person still on duty was Mr. Dickson, the chamber president. He was quite helpful and too polite to be overly nosy about her questions. She thanked him and promised to drop in again.

"Perhaps next time she will be more talkative," he said aloud to himself. He sure hoped so. "Lots of new folk in town these days, and most of 'em asking lots of questions."

What a strange day this has been, thought Elizabeth as she made her way out of the parking space. She really needed to find a place of solitude to try to process all that had transpired. She remembered a park just at the edge of town. Parking near the little gazebo, she lingered several minutes before getting out. Just as she started to open the door, a car whipped past her.

"Wow, that could have literally taken my door off! Thank You, Lord, that I hadn't opened it yet."

For some reason she was more shaken from this event than she realized. The car had screeched to a halt under a big oak tree on the other side of the park. Elizabeth could easily see the driver as she jumped out. The car! The same little sports car that she had seen at the Cozy Corner, and it had parked directly behind another familiar one; the one that the secretive young woman had driven to the motel.

As Elizabeth sat motionless in her car, the driver from the sports car stepped quickly to the sedan and got in. From just the way she moved Elizabeth could tell she was a woman on a mission. Her thin, toned body smartly dressed in an expensive business suit spoke of wealth and purpose. She really looked out of place in this quaint little town—as if she would be more at home on Wall Street or Madison Avenue.

This is absolutely none of my business, Elizabeth thought. She felt embarrassed, as if she had been snooping or spying on some private meeting. Quickly she picked up her briefcase and purse and walked to the gazebo. Once seated inside, listening to the gentle trickling water of the nearby stream, she became composed. Laying the papers from the courthouse out in front of her, she began double checking her list. She had gotten everything Kendra had told her, but she certainly didn't understand much of what she was perusing. She made some notes on a legal pad, trying to recall as much as she could from the afternoon. She jotted down little facts about the Jamison house and property. Doc had told her that although the house had been pretty well kept up, there were several things that were dated. There were some minor electrical and plumbing issues, as one might expect in a house this old. But he had put a new roof on for his grandparents about five years ago, and he knew that the whole house was structurally sound.

Before she knew it the sun had begun to set. How long had she been sitting here? Twisting and stretching, Elizabeth stood up and gazed at the beauty before her. The sun was slowly slipping down behind the ridge. As she watched, it seemed to be sliding from the top of an enormous oak tree; slowly sliding down, it peeked through the bushy limbs, and then it was gone. Even then, the darkness was not disconcerting but actually peaceful and comforting. *Oh, I must go,* she thought. *Those children will be sending out a search party.*

As she gathered her things, she glanced toward where the two curious young women and their cars had been. Neither was there now. When had they left? She realized she had been so engrossed in her own thoughts she had been unaware of anything that went on around her. She had often chided herself for her lack of observation. She thought she was doing better in that area, but she had royally blown it today.

It took only a few minutes to reach the parsonage. As she parked in front, she could see Bill and Carol sitting in the porch swing. The gentle motion and soft creaking seemed to say, "We're here just waiting for you." Again, she was filled with questions. How many times had God used the porch swing and the sounds of nature at dusk to clear the mind and calm the spirit of His man? She really didn't want to intrude.

"Evening, Ms. Elizabeth." In unison they stood and welcomed her. "Ready for supper?"

"Please don't tell me I kept you from your evening meal," Elizabeth exclaimed. "I am so sorry. You should not have waited."

"No, no, really, we didn't. The roast is just now out of the oven, and the biscuits are ready to go in. We were just enjoying the cool and quiet of this beautiful evening. Don't get to do that a lot."

With that, Bill held the door open, and they all entered to be met by an incredibly tantalizing aroma. Only then did Elizabeth realize how hungry she was. She hurried to her room to freshen up and on returning found the table set and waiting. They enjoyed the delicious meal, sharing small talk as old friends do. Very subtly they all seemed to be steering away from any conversation pertaining to the earlier events of the day. It was only after Elizabeth lay on her bed in the darkness of the night that she allowed herself to ponder those thoughts.

Right Prevails

Before dawn, Elizabeth, Bible in hand, stole quietly from her room and moved catlike across the cool wood floor of the living room and out to the porch. She sat motionless in the old swing, knowing that any movement would bring from it the familiar creaking. She did not want to disturb the sleeping pair just inside. Watching the glorious arrival of the light of day was something that she knew would bring her joy and peace. In times past she seldom got up before dawn, but just about everything in her life was different now, and as she often said, most of those differences, strangely enough, were better. As she watched the big yellow ball inch its way into the day, she sat in awe. Nowhere in the universe was autumn any more glorious than in these majestic mountains. She knew other places held God's beauty, but here in the Blue Ridge just as in her beloved Great Smokies she found beauty, peace, and contentment. As the rising sun kissed the leaves of the poplar, maple, and oaks, they danced and swayed and seemed to be paying honor and homage to their Creator. Here, she bowed and worshipped. In her heart, she quietly thanked God for showing Himself to her in this way. As she opened her Bible with humble anticipation, she relinquished herself to Him and His leading for the day.

When the aroma of freshly brewing coffee and the sound of sizzling bacon reached her, Elizabeth rose from her place of worship. Carol was startled when she heard the door open.

"Good morning. I had no idea you were up already."

"Oh, I've been up for a while. I hope I didn't disturb you. I was just enjoying the porch swing and this beautiful morning. Letting the new morning light illuminate the Word for me just seemed the right thing to do." Elizabeth laid her Bible on the counter and asked if she could be of any help.

"Sure," answered Carol. "Maybe you could get the jelly and butter and juice from the 'fridge. Biscuits almost done. All I got to do now is scramble some eggs. As you already know, I don't do biscuits and gravy and all this every day, but Bill loves a big breakfast. I think surely just once a week won't totally wreck his cholesterol."

As Carol handed Elizabeth a cup of freshly brewed coffee, she noticed that she was giving her the same cup that she had used every time since she had arrived here. That gesture alone made her feel as if she were part of their family. Funny how each person always seems to have a favorite cup or place at the table. Elizabeth smiled.

Bill, yawning and looking just like a college kid in his jeans and T-shirt, entered. "Boy, I hope not," he said as he winked at Elizabeth and gave his wife a tender squeeze. "But if that kind of breakfast kills me, at least I will die a happy man."

As they enjoyed a leisurely breakfast, both Bill and Carol told Elizabeth about their lives before coming to Leesboro and how much they loved the people of this sleepy little village. Elizabeth was surprised to learn that they were both military brats and as such had traveled the world. Each had come home for college:

Bill to VMI and Carol to Liberty. They each had felt God's calling to go into full-time Christian service. They had met at a crusade at Liberty and started a long-distance courtship. After Bill graduated and just before he left for active duty, he asked Carol to marry him. She told Elizabeth she did not see at that time how being a military wife would put her into Christian service, but she loved Bill and knew she was to accept his proposal. They had been happy with military life but knew there was something more ahead for them. With family members not understanding at all, they left the Navy and Bill entered seminary. He had accepted the call to Leesboro immediately after graduation and had been here ever since.

"I'd like to say we found ourselves and our place, but the truth is, God brought us to the place He had planned for us all along." Bill spoke with such conviction that tears began to well in Elizabeth's eyes. She knew he was right.

After helping Carol with the cleanup, Elizabeth went in to get ready to go into town to meet Franklin and Kendra. Waiting for them, she again looked at some of the documents. "I am so thankful, Lord, to have the Laytons to go with me through this," she said aloud, "and You in control of it all."

It was only a little after eleven when Elizabeth saw Franklin's vintage Mustang pull up in front of the courthouse. "Best place to meet," Kendra had said. "Franklin can find the courthouse in any town."

"Greetings, m'lady," bellowed Franklin as they came toward her. Elizabeth hugged them both before steering them toward the diner. "Let's have coffee and decide what we need to do first," she said.

Just seeing her two dear friends gave her great comfort. She had complete confidence in how they would handle her needs. They were both excellent lawyers, as knowledgeable and competent as anyone she knew when it came to real estate law. Not only that, but they were long-time Christian friends. Her oldest brother and Franklin's uncle had grown up together, had gone to war together, and had even gone to college together after returning. It was a running joke that doctors and lawyers were supposed to be enemies, but Lawyer Laython and Doctor Barrington were as close as any friends could ever be. It was inevitable that Franklin Laython Sr. would be legal counsel for the Barringtons, and when Franklin Jr. had joined the firm, he was the one Elizabeth had turned to.

Just as they were leaving the diner, they were hailed by Adele and Denton Curry. Franklin looked as if he had seen a ghost.

"Dent? Dent Curry?" He gasped. "Is that really you?"

Elizabeth and Kendra stared at each other in amazement. "You two know each other," Elizabeth finally asked. By now the two men were laughing, hugging, patting each other on the backs, and generally acting in a very uncivilized manner.

"Whoa! Hold on," Adele yelled. "What is going on with you two mad men?"

Denton finally composed himself and spoke, "Well," he started, grinning from ear to ear. "Ole Franklin here was my law school partner way back yonder in another life. We lost touch when we left Duke, and I went west to *find myself*. Ever since I came back, I intended to look him up but just never did. Man, I can't believe this! How did we manage to run into each other in this little place?"

"I'm Elizabeth's realtor," Adele broke in, "and Denton's wife, Adele. Denton has told me a little about those days of long ago—and some of your exploits—but this is just unbelievable!"

"Since we need to get on over to the Jamisons', we'll just car pool," stated Denton. "You girls pile in together with Adele, and

I'll ride shotgun with ole Frankie, boy. Maybe you should just let me drive, Frankie, since you don't know the road and all, huh?"

"That's quite all right, Dent, ole boy. I can follow your directions just fine. I still remember that lead foot of yours!"

"Do you think we can expect them to make it to the farm? They are acting completely giddy," Adele said. "I have never seen my husband act this way."

"Nor I," chimed in Kendra, "but I'm hoping I'm right when I say that surely they are still the responsible, mature men we know!"

Elizabeth slid into the seat behind Adele, allowing Kendra the front passenger seat. Kendra was already asking questions that could be best answered by Adele. For most of the short ride Elizabeth remained quiet, thinking more than talking, not even really listening to the conversation from the front seat. Once or twice Kendra glanced back with a questioning look but didn't say anything until they got out of the car.

"Elizabeth," she said quietly. "Liddy, are you okay? Is something wrong?"

Adele went on in front to join the men, leaving Elizabeth and Kendra to walk alone.

"No, nothing really," Elizabeth answered pensively. "I guess I am just once again trying to figure out what God is doing. You would think by now I would have learned not to do that, wouldn't you? He is not obligated to explain His steps to me. But I can tell you one thing, He is at work here and all that is going on is much bigger than just my situation."

Doc was waiting on the porch for them, and after the introductions were made he invited them in.

"Oh, Liddy," exclaimed Kendra, "this is the picture you painted in my mind a long time ago. This is just too surreal."

Elizabeth knew Franklin would be very cautious with his words and would study every aspect of the house and every concept of the idea before saying much. She valued the input from each of them and knew they were there to represent her best interests. As they once again moved from room to room, Franklin asked pertinent questions, some being answered by Denton, others by Doc.

Tomorrow after church they would walk the land even though they could already see that the lay was conducive to walking trails, picnic areas, and the like. Elizabeth did want to see the little falls that Joe Bob had told her about. *"They are down there where the cedars sing,"* he had said. That statement had intrigued her, and she felt drawn to seek them out.

After hours and hours of talking, walking, discussing, and figuring, they called it a day. Completely exhausted Elizabeth went to her room immediately after Sunday night service.

When Elizabeth awoke the next morning, she was amazed to find that she was had slept so well. She felt rested, refreshed, and even excited to face the day. Soon, with Pastor Bill and Carol by her side, she headed to their car.

"Oh, you children don't need to do this," she stated. "I will be fine. My attorney will meet me."

"Now, Ms. Elizabeth," Bill began. "We are going to take you to the courthouse. We will pray as we drive along." He patted her hand, then linked arms with her and Carol. The decision had been made. Bill held the door for her as she got out, and then with a hug that was more like one from a son than a preacher, they said good-bye.

The next thing she knew, she, along with Franklin and Kendra, were being directed to their seats at a conference table in the Leesboro courthouse. At first glance, it appeared that the whole town had turned out for this meeting: a judge; Mr.

Williams, the Register of Deeds; Doc and Anna Louise; and the Currys. She soon learned that the two men on the other side of the table were the ones who held the note on the Jamison property. Elizabeth got the distinct impression that they were there to take possession of *their* property.

When the judge opened the meeting, he asked the men if they understood that the Jamisons still had the right to pay off the note and retain the property. One of them spoke with what could only be described as a sneer. "Oh, yes, your honor! We understand that perfectly—but do *you* see the amount of money we are talking about here?"

Elizabeth tried not to fidget in her chair. Out of the corner of her eye, she could see Doc clenching his jaw and tears welling in Anna Louise's eyes. Had they been wrong? Was there enough money to handle the deal after all?

"I assure you, Mr. Creighton, I am well aware of the figure. Mr. Williams has presented me with all the documentation I need. Now, I have here a cashier's check, so if you will hand over the note, we will make it PAID IN FULL and you can be on your way!"

"What! You can *not* be serious! We came here to claim our property! You can't do this!" Both men jumped to their feet.

"*Sit down*, both of you!" Judge Thorton bellowed. Only then did Elizabeth realize a side door had opened and the sheriff had slipped in.

"Your ugly scheme has backfired, and your game is over. You may accept the check quietly as you hand over the note, or you may not; it really matters not at all to me. This is a binding legal action, and it is over. The Jamisons retain possession. And by the way, the district attorney has been made aware of your shenanigans here as well as in Atlanta. You will be hearing from several other officers of the court!"

Mr. Williams, in his official capacity as register of deeds, finalized the remaining business under the watchful eye of Judge Thorton. And it was over! The two "businessmen from Atlanta," red-faced and angry, could not get out of the room quickly enough.

Sheriff Contrell grinned as he closed the door behind them. "Don't worry, they are not going far. Federal marshals are waiting outside with a stack of warrants and two pairs of handcuffs."

"Okay, Ms. Barrington, we will now move on. Your attorney has given me your check for the back taxes and the one dollar you are paying the Jamisons. In return they will sign the property over to you. You will then give them a one hundred–year lease for the cabin."

All the details were clear to Elizabeth, but she still could hardly believe it. Even Judge Thorton was somewhat amazed as to how it had all come together. It was he who said that this was one for the books and that a higher power had orchestrated it. Elizabeth knew that. Her only response was … *"What now?"*

Time for Celebration

Leaving the courthouse with a heart so full and so light, Elizabeth felt as if she were floating on the billowy white clouds overhead. The noonday sun kissed the autumn leaves as they danced their way through the gentle breeze on their way to the ground. Could there ever be a day as beautiful, as perfect as this?

The little entourage moved slowly and silently down the massive stone steps as if collectively they feared any minute they might awaken from this unbelievable dream. Just a few days earlier they had almost succumbed to defeat. Now, a whole new horizon lay before them. Of course, it was somewhat daunting for both Elizabeth and the Jamison family but nonetheless, uplifting and exciting.

Reaching the bottom step, Elizabeth turned as if by fate to see a car pulling away from the curb, coming toward them. She was in no danger, but instinctively she stepped back, all the while staying focused on the occupants. *How strange,* she thought. *Those are the two women I saw in the park a few days ago.* They both stared at the group now on the sidewalk beside her, glaring menacingly.

"Liddy," Kendra whispered as she touched Elizabeth's arm. "Who are those two, and why were they looking at us that way?"

"I don't know the answer to either question, Kendra, but I have seen them before. They sure look out of place here, don't they?" Suddenly a light came on for Elizabeth! The girl, the younger one at the wheel, she knew where she had first encountered her. It was at the home of Mrs. Bea the day she and Adele had stopped to see about her piece of property that they thought was on the market. This was the granddaughter who had quickly told them it had already been sold and rushed them away.

"Oh, dear," Elizabeth gasped, "she's also the one I saw so secretively going into Cozy Corner! What on earth does all this mean? Have I in some strange way stumbled into … something? But if so, what?"

Adele, too, had recognized the girl. Turning to her husband, she said only to him, "I've got a bad feeling about all this. I think we need to go check on Mrs. Bea, but we need not alarm anyone. Let's just give some excuse and hurry on over there."

"Okay," Denton replied. Not knowing what was going on did not keep him from reacting. He had long ago learned to trust his wife's intuition. "Uh," he whispered, "just go with me on this."

As if by divine intervention, Anna Louise spoke, "If all of you will, just go on out to the house where I'm sure by now a picnic is spread. I didn't want to mention it earlier, in case something …" She let the sentence drop. "Pastor Bill and Carol came out to be with Joe Bob, and they are preparing a celebration picnic. Guess they had more faith than I. I am sure glad they were right!"

Denton took his cue. "Great! Adele and I must run one quick errand, but we'll join you just as soon as we can. You go on. Don't wait for us, just leave us a morsel or two." With that, he laughed heartily, grabbed Adele by the hand, and headed to the Jeep before anyone could respond.

"Okay then, Ms. Elizabeth, bring your friends—our new friends—and let's go see what they have cooked up for us," Doc said. Anyone could easily see that the weariness on his face had been replaced with a look of relief and peace. Franklin couldn't help but think that here was a deep thinker, one who took the heavy responsibility of caring for his sister and brother very seriously.

"I imagine," Franklin said to himself, "that everything about this young man is deep. Our Liddy is going to be just fine in this place."

As was almost always the case, Joe Bob was beside the cars before they had completely stopped. "Hello, Sister," he said as he grabbed Anna Louise. "You been gone a long time. I missed you, but I helped Miss Carol and Pastor Bill real good just like I help you."

"Oh, I know you did, sweetie. Thank you so much. You are just the best helper around."

The way Anna Louise dealt with Joe Bob was simply and absolutely love in action. Anyone who cared to look could easily see that her care, concern, and love for him came from the most sincere heart. She embraced his specialness in such a way that Elizabeth wished the world at large could learn. She silently thanked God for having brought her here … to this beautiful part of the world and to these beautiful people!

Joe Bob took his sister by one hand and Elizabeth by the other and began to drag them toward the big table in the yard. It was laden down with picnic fare: fried chicken, green beans, corn on the cob, potato salad, coleslaw, even fresh hot yeast rolls straight from the oven.

"Good grief, Doc, do you eat this way every day?" Franklin asked with astonishment. "I'd weigh four hundred pounds if I did."

"No, not every day he doesn't, Mr. Laython," Pastor Bill said as he extended his hand. "I'm Bill Vance. His sister and my wife don't cook like this for just ordinary guys like us." He laughed as he gave his wife a playful squeeze. "They just try to impress city folk any time they get a chance."

"Well, they've certainly done so today. I'm impressed. I first thought maybe we should wait for Dent and his wife, but I've changed my mind on that. I'm gonna dive in before they get here; I've been at the table with Dent Curry before!"

Everyone laughed, and Elizabeth thought how wonderful this fellowship was—old friends and new, and she felt so at home. They joined hands around the table. Not only did the young pastor ask for God's blessing, he ushered all of them into a time of thanksgiving for the abundant blessings of this day.

They had enjoyed such a pleasant time of fellowship that they had just begun to take their seats with overly filled plates when Denton and Adele drove up. Joe Bob ran to meet them in his usual manner, bringing them quickly to the table.

"We already said grace, Mr. Denton, Miss Adele, so just dig in," he said as he carefully chose a plate for each of them. "I know you both like Miss Carol's tea so I'll get you each a glass. I'll put a lemon in yours, Miss Adele."

Elizabeth watched as he so adeptly used the tongs to place three ice cubes in a red cup for Adele, a blue one for Denton. He painstakingly poured the tea, spilling not a drop. Only after he had replaced the cover on the pitcher did he place a lemon wedge in Adele's cup. He showed them where they should sit, placing their cups at exactly the correct places. He might just as well have been carrying antique crystal goblets with all the care he was taking. Only after he checked to make sure he had properly covered the lemon bowl and placed it back precisely where it had been, did he return to his seat.

Just as Carol began to serve banana pudding, Denton leaned his elbows on the table and spoke.

"Everybody, Adele and I have a real story to tell!"

Not a sound could be heard. It seemed that all of nature stopped, hovered, waiting.

SINISTER PLOTS REVEALED

"**G**et comfortable," he went on. "This is gonna knock your socks off! That little errand we had to run ... well, that was out to Mrs. Bea's place. Ms. Elizabeth, I could see that you recognized those women in the car back in town just as Adele did. The younger was Marcie, Mrs. Bea's granddaughter. But you didn't know the other one, did you?"

"No, I didn't know her, but I have seen her before."

"Well, this is just kicker number *one*! That sophisticated *lady* was none other than Donna Lee Davis, Doc's long-ago girlfriend!"

"What?" Doc almost screamed! "What are you talking about? When did you see her ... them, I mean? I'm really not following any of this."

"Neither are any of the rest of us, Doc," Bill said quietly.

Anna Louise and Carol were staring first at Denton, then at Doc. Joe Bob had already gone to the cabin to take his afternoon nap. Doc and Anna Louise were both glad that Denton had waited until he left to begin his saga. They knew Joe Bob often became agitated when he didn't understand the conversation or if he sensed that something might be upsetting someone, and they felt pretty sure this was going to be one of those times.

Here Adele picked up the story.

"One of the first days Elizabeth and I went out land searching we drove over to Mrs. Bea's place. Marcie was there, and she was *not* happy to see us. She informed us in a hurry that her grandmother's land had already been sold. She thought she got Mrs. Bea away from us before we could learn any more, but she didn't quite do it. Remember that wink and quick word Mrs. Bea gave me, Elizabeth? Well, here is where it really gets good. You pick it up here, honey, and let me get my breath."

Denton did just that. "Okay, well. I guess you might know that I have handled Mrs. Bea's legal matters for years. Actually, she was my very first client, so I know almost as much about her business affairs as she does. Let me tell you this: that old lady is a sly one. I sure wouldn't want to be on the other side of any deal where she is concerned.

"But anyway, little Miss Smarty-Pants Marcie thought that she and some of her unsavory cohorts had pulled a fast one on Mrs. Bea and gotten her to sign her property over to Marcie. She was just trying to get rid of Adele and Elizabeth by telling them that it had already been sold. Mrs. Bea probably thought at the time that Adele knew better, but of course, she didn't."

"Okay, Denton, I'm following you so far, but how does Donna Lee fit in this?" Doc asked.

"Oh, she's the one who put the whole ugly plan in motion. Doc, I'm so glad God saved you from that one. More than likely she has already been picked up and thrown in jail with … and get this … those two guys we just dealt with!"

The more they heard of the tangled web, the more astounded they were. All around the table heads were shaking and eyes were growing wider and wider. Elizabeth had no history with any of these people, so she was able to view everything from a little different perspective, but even she was now in shock. She knew God had led her this way, but she thought it was only for her benefit. Now she was seeing that she was only one small player in the entire situation. She leaned closer to Denton, not wanting to miss a single word. She glanced at Doc. He looked petrified, but he urged Denton to continue.

"Donna Lee knew that your land shared a line with Mrs. Bea's, Doc. She planned to get both pieces and turn it into a resort center ... with gambling parlors and all kinds of ungodly enterprises. Remember where you showed me that you had planned to build the house for you and her, Doc. She had a real deal planned for that—a really upscale hotel with *ladies* taking care of all the business there. The big guys from Atlanta had access to money to develop it. They had gone all the way to getting the permits for all they were planning. I'm sure it goes without saying that they had some people in high places in their pockets."

Here again Adele jumped in.

"Marcie was just dumb enough to think she would have a prestigious position and plenty of money when all this came together. She had no concern at all for the dear lady who took her in and raised her. She has been so involved with drugs and alcohol and the people who move in those circles that her whole brain is fried. She doesn't see yet that she may have just been saved from an overdose death in some back alley, compliments of her *friends*."

"Please," Anna Louise said pleadingly. "Tell us how Mrs. Bea's part of this came out. Is she okay?"

"Oh, honey, that is one of the best parts," Adele said, laughing. "But Denton is going to have to tell you that. I'm still trying to sort it all out. I think you'll find that I have a brilliant husband here," she said as she patted Denton on the back.

"It was actually Mrs. Bea who was the smart one. She was so on top of everything that she protected herself and her land long before Marcie started her devilish business. She called me to come out to discuss some important matters long before your grandmother passed away. You know how close they always were and how she loved your mom and dad. She told me she had put Joe Bob in her will just days after he was born. She wanted to make sure he always had whatever he needed."

"Take a little break, Denton," Bill said. "Let's get this table cleared and make some coffee. I can tell we are going to be here for a while."

"Yes, good idea, Pastor. We just couldn't wait to tell you this story. Sounds like a Lifetime or Hallmark tale, doesn't it?"

Anxious to hear the next chapter, everyone began gathering up food and clearing the table. In a very short time they finished up and were again seated around the table with mugs of steaming hot coffee.

"All right, Dent," Franklin Layton said, "I know none of these people really, but I wouldn't want to miss a single word of this. This is the most intriguing thing I have heard in many a day. Hon, our lives with pencil pushers and corporate mergers are going to seem awfully dull after this."

"Okay, where did I get?"

"You were telling about Mrs. Bea and her provision for Joe Bob." Anna Louise wanted him to get right back on track. She still couldn't believe that part.

"Yes," Denton began. "At her death, Joe Bob is to inherit the original house and the acreage behind it that touches his grandparents' property. The rest is to go to the church with the stipulation that it is never to be sold. She would like to see the big house used as a mission house and a place for Christian couples' retreats. She has given me permission to tell all of you this, but there is much more than just what I sharing today. You would not believe the vision that dear old saint has."

"What?" both Doc and Anna Louise said simultaneously.

"You are not serious," Doc gasped.

"I have never been more serious. Mrs. Bea knows exactly what she wants, and she has already done it. As for the documents she signed for Marcie, they aren't worth the paper they are written on. She had me draw up some bogus papers, and greedy Marcie didn't bother to read any fine print. Some might question our tactics, but I assure you we would not and did not do anything illegal. A very shrewd old lady just clipped the wings of an evil little girl right in front of her."

After a long silence, Elizabeth hesitantly spoke. "If that is all, I want to ask a couple of questions."

Denton nodded. "Yes, except for a lot of legal mumbo-jumbo that is the whole thing in a nutshell. So go right ahead."

"Well, then. What I want to know is, do I really own this wonderful house and land? Is it mine as long as I live or choose to sell it back to the Jamisons? And do I really have them as my lifelong neighbors?"

Doc reached for her hand. "Those are easy questions to answer, Ms. Elizabeth. One word: *yes*! And we are the blessed ones in this whole deal."

Elizabeth, through tear-filled eyes, looked at her friends, old and new, and saw that they too were wiping tears. She wanted to say something, but no words would come. She slowly stood and walked across the yard to the old apple tree. The cool breeze of an autumn day was settling in on the most picturesque scene. The sun would soon be setting, earlier than yesterday, she thought.

"Please God," she whispered. "Let me forever keep this day, this moment. And please show me some way to express my gratefulness both to You and to these people."

Peace Fields

Elizabeth had begun this phase of her life journey at the time of Indian summer, and now she was settling in just before winter's end. So much had transpired since her first trip to Leesboro. There is no way human reasoning can understand the working of the omniscient God. Would that she could just learn to accept.

It seemed to her that all of Leesboro had tried to help with the monumental tasks that lay before her. Doc and Denton had spearheaded the efforts of finding the best people possible to tackle each task. Together, they had helped her lay out a plan to accomplish all that must be done. She had told them of the time frame she believed to be right, and they were driven to help her reach it. Fortunately, most of the work was just time consuming, not major tearing out or rebuilding. The house had all the charm of a once-magnificent home, and she wanted none of that altered in any way. A house that is truly a home is something to be cherished, and that was her passion.

They had bathed each new challenge in prayer and even in her absence had begun the work. Often, during the early winter months she had planned trips from North Carolina, but almost every one of them had been thwarted. Each time that had happened, she had turned her energies to moving from her old life and preparing for the new. She had heard many young missionaries talk about what they had done in preparing for their fields of service in strange new lands. She knew her situation was completely different, but she found herself applying their methods anyway. And it was working. She was not leaving things behind; she was willingly and joyfully casting much aside. She would take with her only what was necessary or in some cases special items she could not bear to be without. Among those were an heirloom quilt, a painting, a teapot, a baby dress with its blue ribbon from a competition ... and the piano. The more of the *casting aside* she did, the lighter felt her heart and spirit. She finally arrived at a place within that brought deep, settled peace. Right direction and right decision were hers, and she would no longer wonder or *wander*.

Before her now lay the new horizon, the clean slate, the yellow brick road that many desire and some even dare to travel. It had been a life-long journey. She many times felt sad that she had not arrived at this place earlier, but she also knew that God's timing was always perfect, and she embraced it enthusiastically. Once again Jeremiah 29:11 flooded her soul. "For I know the thoughts that I think toward you, saith the LORD, thoughts of peace, and not of evil, to give you an expected end." How she loved the Word of God. The one constant in her life had been her relationship with Him.

She felt much younger now than her *mature years* as she focused not so much on walking away from one life as happily running toward another. Each new step seemed to heighten her anticipation for whatever was before her; much as a child who is told to "open your eyes now and see your gift."

Doc and the people he had found to help with the work at Cedar Grove had made remarkable progress. Elizabeth was now sure that as the days grew warmer, the flower beds and gardens would themselves speak of their needs. Joe Bob had lovingly begun the task of clearing away the debris and laying down new borders. He had followed his sister's instructions to the letter in putting in scores of bulbs last fall. Elizabeth continued to be amazed at the talents of Anna Louise. In the short time that she had known her, she had seen the sense of pride in any task she began.

"A rare jewel, this one," Elizabeth mused. "She exemplifies the scripture ... *do all to the glory of God.*"

The residents of Leesboro had opened their arms and hearts to Elizabeth as if she had always been one of their own. She hadn't been sure how they might feel about the business she envisioned in their quiet rural community. Much to her joy they seemed to be as excited as she. The *Leesboro Weekly* continually informed its readers of the progress with "our newest neighbor, Cedar Grove Bed and Breakfast." Elizabeth had even been invited to speak at the March town hall meeting. She had gladly accepted and was daily making notes as to what she would need to say.

1. Cedar Grove is a small (four-bedroom) bed and breakfast
2. Elaborate on the charm of the house and grounds
3. Rooms reasonably priced
4. Christian-based business/ministry
5. *Possibly, occasionally* host some catered events
6. The picnic area beyond the creek would be available for church-related youth meetings/retreats.

Here, Elizabeth stopped and reflected on the stories the Jamisons had shared with her about Peace Fields, as Gramma Jamison had called it.

It seemed in the early days of their marriage Mrs. Jamison noticed her young husband was slipping away quite early in the mornings ... before sunrise ... returning just before she came down to prepare breakfast. He followed a pattern. As she entered the big country kitchen, he would greet her with an affectionate hug and kiss and state, "I've got the stove going; coffee just about ready. Sit yourself down and have a cup 'fore you get started."

Days grew into weeks with no change in the routine. Occasionally she would make some little joke, asking if he had a mistress in the barn, hoping he would give some hint of his actions. He would only chuckle and assure her she was his one and only. They were so much in love she knew that to be true. As summer melted into fall, she became almost obsessed with not knowing what was going on. When her birthday came and went, she knew he had not secretly been working on some special gift for her.

One morning Anna could stand it no longer. This time when C. J. slipped down the stairs and out the back door, she was peeking from the window. She watched as he left the yard, walking swiftly toward the creek. The underbrush was so thick he was gone from her sight in only a moment. She quickly threw aside her nightgown and donned old pants and shirt and her heavy work boots. She hurried down the path and through the woods. Not really liking the thought of what one might encounter, she seldom ever ventured off the familiar paths; but this morning she had to see!

She moved as quietly and stealthily as possible, not wanting to be detected in her quest. She had no idea where he had gone ... or how far. She was nearing the creek when she heard a voice. His voice. It was low, soft, and gentle. He was crooning, singing in what could only be described as a worshipful way. Anna realized she had never really heard him sing before, at least not this way. Tears filled her eyes. She parted the brush just enough to get a glimpse of him. She remained motionless and silent, drinking in the scene and enjoying the moment.

As C. J. moved on a bit farther, so did Anna. Now, with a better view, she had to cover her mouth to keep from gasping loud enough to be heard. Before her she clearly saw what had taken him from her all those mornings. He had built an altar and a sanctuary—a place for worship. Across the creek was a humpback cedar bridge; beyond it a huge clearing with a soft carpet of grass. Wildflowers, flame azaleas, and enormous rhododendron served as a protective wall all around. At one end was a stone fireplace and at the other an altar also of stone that had been carried from the creek. So carefully placed were they that one might think an artist had designed the erecting. Huge evergreens were all around as if watching over the sacred place. Anna had seen places of natural beauty and even pictures by renowned painters, but nothing could compare with what her eyes and her heart were now beholding. Watching her young husband bowing before the altar, she could restrain herself no longer.

She pushed her way through the brush and ran across the little bridge, waving and crying and yelling. Bewildered, C. J. turned from the altar just in time to catch her as she fell into his arms. "Oh, C. J.!" she screamed. "This is the most beautiful place I have ever seen! How did you do all this? And why?"

As they sank to the ground, still holding each other, he spoke. He seemed almost embarrassed as he told her he had been working on this place of sanctuary for her—for the two of them.

"I know as we travel life's road together, there will be days of difficulty, times of questions with no answers, times when a place of solitude will be necessary. This is where God has led me."

They sat on the cool ground for quite some time enjoying each other with the beauty of nature surrounding them. As they listened to the soothing sounds of water falling over the miniature falls Robert had uncovered, the birds filled the morning air with their beautiful songs. The many sounds of God's creation were all around them. Anna wondered if this might be what Eden had been like.

After a time of reverence and worship, they joined arms and reluctantly left their private place. On the bridge, Anna turned and with glistening eyes said a simple, sweet thank you to her adoring husband. "This wonderful sanctuary will be here long after we're gone, dearest. You've provided a place for generations of children and grandchildren to steal away to, and they will be blessed because of your labor of love."

Anna Louise and Doc had told Elizabeth that they were brought here often by their parents and grandparents. Many nights were spent sleeping under a glorious canopy of stars, listening to nature's night music. Scores of young people from Leesboro Baptist had come for times of study and retreat. It indeed was a place of worship, and Elizabeth intended for it to continue to be.

Not a lot more would need to be said at the town meeting, for all of Leesboro knew much of her intended plan. In the past that might have irritated Elizabeth, but somehow in this place it just seemed right. The people here were genuinely open and honest and very unpretentious, so Elizabeth was comfortable with them knowing her plans. Many of them had prayed with her, worked alongside her, and were now rejoicing with her as her big day was fast approaching. On Sunday, Pastor Bill would extend an invitation to everyone to an open house at Cedar Grove on the following Saturday, just one week before Easter. More than a little nervous, Elizabeth hoped she would be ready.

The Laythons would be coming for the gala affair. They, too, had fallen in love with Leesboro and had come as often as possible over the last few weeks. Franklin and Denton had reestablished their old college relationship, and their wives were becoming fast friends.

Anna Louise had designed some charming brochures and posters using hand-drawn pictures of each room in the house. Elizabeth had consulted with Janice from the Cozy Corner about the best colors to use throughout the house. Much of the decorating had been dictated by what was already in the house. This had been a house built by the hands of a loving husband and father and kept by a wife and mother who had given herself completely to those who lived here, those whom she loved. Working together, they had taken the beautiful house and made it a home. Using that as her starting point, Elizabeth was confident about each step she took.

Kendra had brought a friend from Charlotte to "show off" what had been done. The friend was so impressed that she wanted to invite a writer/friend from *Southern Living* to come up and do a feature story on Cedar Grove. Elizabeth declined her offer "until perhaps a later time." She selfishly wanted to keep Leesboro a bit of a secret just a little while longer. *This life here is too special to be inundated with greedy types who would destroy our serenity*, she thought.

Almost every day Elizabeth awoke to find Joe Bob hard at work in the yard. He removed every weed from every flowerbed, checked every rock in every border to make sure it hadn't shifted ... since yesterday. He put out safe repellents to keep "the bunnies and squirrels and even little Bambies away." "I don't want to hurt them, Ms. Liz-beth," he would tell her. "I'll take them some food way down yonder in the woods. I just don't want them to eat your pretty flowers."

He had trimmed every bush and every shrub with painstaking care. With Doc's help he had built some circular benches around two of the oak trees. Elizabeth knew how the beautiful grounds would draw people. She also knew she could never adequately compensate Joe Bob for all he done, though on several occasions she had offered. He seemed offended.

"Oh, no, Ms. Liz-beth, I don't want that! I love my Gramma and Grandpa's house, and I love you. They let me do stuff like this 'fore they went to heaven, and they would want me to do it for you now. You're not gonna go to heaven soon too, are you?" In his eyes she could see a love and sincerity unlike any other that she had ever seen. How very, very special he was. She learned more and more each day as to why Doc and Anna Louise called him their angel.

"No, I don't plan to go right away, Joe Bob," she assured him. "But one day! Maybe you and I can just go at the same time someday." He smiled, gave her a big squeeze with his stubby little arms and soil-covered hands, and went back to his task, singing all the while.

Being a planner and a list maker, as opening day drew closer, Elizabeth began to make notes as she moved from room to room.

1. Exchange chair in parlor with one from my room.
2. Reposition picture in downstairs powder room.
3. Replace floral decanter with crystal one in room number one.

On and on she went, trying to make sure every aspect of the decorating and arranging was pleasant, inviting, and would have a calming, comforting effect on her as she entered each room. She knew if that worked for her, it would work for her guests as well. Throughout the house she had placed books and magazines and even stationery and pads and pens.

One of her personal favorite items to place in each room was a water fountain carefully chosen with just the right colors and theme. In the king room with its antique lace ecru coverlet she had placed one that had miniature figures enjoying a garden tea party.

The subtle shades of mauve and dusty rose were the inspiration for all the other accents in the room. The water trickled down tiny rows of translucent beads while a hidden music box played the gentle strains of "The Blue Danube Waltz."

In the foyer, just inside the massive antique oak doors, she had placed a large fountain that spilled over into a pond of water flowers. At night its low lights cast captivating shadows on the walls. Often she stood before it just listening to the rippling water and the methodic ticking of the enormous grandfather clock in the corner. Here, too, was a large marble-topped library table on which she kept an ancient family Bible and a vase of fresh flowers. More often than not, yellow roses filled her cherished Blue Willow vase. She always tucked in some little sprigs of lavender or eucalyptus or mint, just enough to give an inviting hint of fragrance. So peaceful and pleasant was this area that she jokingly said to herself that she should just throw a pillow and a quilt on the floor and sleep there. *Only on the hottest nights would that work*, she thought. *That flagstone floor can be awfully cold!*

Being so busy with final preparations, Elizabeth had not spent much time with friends lately. Both Adele and Carol had stopped by on several occasions but had not lingered. Each of them had already learned enough about their new friend to know that she preferred to entertain only when she was not preoccupied.

Preparation

At the end of service on Sunday when Pastor Bill made the formal announcement of the opening and extended Elizabeth's invitation, everyone cheered. So many had been involved in the whole process that they felt a degree of ownership in the joy. As Elizabeth expected might be the case, she was bombarded with offers of help— everything from bringing food to helping serve and clean up. Although she acknowledged every kind gesture and graciously tried to decline, she knew no one was listening. Many would be there long before the two o'clock dedication hour, laden down with their famous dishes; and they would be there long after all the casual visitors and well-wishers were gone.

Her friends were all so giving, and she knew that God was teaching her to be a receiver. He was showing her that she must lay aside pride and allow Him to bless others as they reached out to help her. That night as she laid in the darkness, she once again called on God to help her. Perhaps more than ever before in her life, she wanted to be a cleansed vessel for Him to use, and she really wanted to empty herself before Him. As a thin finger of moonlight sliced through the opening in the curtain and laid itself on her breast she fell asleep with that prayer on her lips, replaying the words of Jeremiah the prophet in Jeremiah 18, about the potter and the clay.

The following week, each day sped into the next with such a flurry of activity that Elizabeth collapsed into her bed at night. It seemed that no sooner had she closed her eyes than she was rudely jarred awake by the invasive clanging of her alarm clock. She had never before even set an alarm, but this week she dared not waste a single moment of precious time.

"Next week," she said aloud as she reluctantly and painfully raised herself from her cocoon of quilts. "Next week, I am going to stay in bed until eleven. Every single day I am going to do that!"

Knowing that would never happen, she smiled and exited her bed, all the while thanking God for a good night's sleep. Only minutes later, Bible in hand, she made her way to the porch to wake up communing with God—and a strong pot of coffee. She planned to invite overnight guests to join her in this ritual if they chose. If not, her serving them would come after. She had long ago made this commitment to both God and herself. It was the nourishment she must have to begin the day and sustain life.

On Thursday when she opened her morning paper, Elizabeth was greeted with a most pleasant surprise. There on the front page was a large color picture of Cedar Grove "with story and pictures inside!" She was stunned. She knew several people had asked to take pictures of the work in progress, but she never dreamed of anything like this. And what a story inside! There was an entire page of pictures, from Joe Bob's wonderfully landscaped grounds to tiny details throughout the house. At the bottom was the story with everything from its history to its restoration. Peter Clayton, owner and publisher, had done the entire story. He ended the article with an announcement of the opening as well as a promise of pictures from the dedication in next week's paper.

My word! No marketing guru could have bought better advertisement than this—and they have given it to me—for free! Her next thought was, *How many people are going to show up for the dedication and grand opening?!* Carefully laying the paper out on the parlor table, she rushed into the kitchen to start making more punch to put in the freezer and more crescent roll dough. Tomorrow she would make multiple recipes of chicken salad and ham delights.

All that day, Elizabeth labored in the kitchen, trying to calm her fears as to the amount of food she should have. She was so glad she had purchased the big double door refrigerator at a restaurant closing sale. It was late when she finally mopped the kitchen floor and put a load of dish towels in to wash, but every inch of 'fridge space was filled to capacity. "Lord, it will just have to be enough," she mused. "I can do no more!" Smiling as she pulled the string to turn off the overhead light, she couldn't get the story of the loaves and fishes out of her exhausted brain.

Just as she was finishing her quiet time on Friday morning, she saw Doc and Bill unloading the tables she had borrowed from the church. Stepping out, she greeted them and thanked them for all their help.

"No problem, Ms. Elizabeth," said the pastor in his boyish, kind voice. "We'll just put them under the shed, and then in the morning we will be here to put them where you want them. Sure hope it's a nice day since you're planning this bash for the outside."

"Yes, me too, Bill, but if it isn't, we'll just go to the porches and inside. I am not going to borrow from tomorrow's trouble today."

"Hey, that'd make for a good sermon, don't you think?" He chuckled and climbed back into the truck. Both he and Doc waved and were on their way.

Back inside, Elizabeth busied herself putting finishing touches on everything. Consulting her "To Do On Friday" list, she checked off item by item as she completed the tasks of the day. She did a final dusting in the foyer and parlor, a last-minute touch-up in each bathroom, making sure everything glistened. She went from room to room, slowly moving around so she could scrutinize from every angle. Here a rug was repositioned, there a pillow was fluffed. Finally, she knew that not one speck of dust could be found, not a single book was out of place.

Just as she was about to fall asleep, she heard the gentle tap, tap, tapping of softly falling rain on the porch roof just outside her window. Rain was always comforting and soothing, but this time she didn't welcome it as joyfully as usual. She was much too tired to dwell on the difficulties that could arise with a saturated lawn. Scarlett would think on that tomorrow!

She didn't know when the rain had stopped, but the bright sunshine and the cloudless day greeted her as she awakened on this all-important day. Every day held its own magic at Cedar Grove, but this one was picture perfect. Last night's rain had gently washed every leaf and every blade of grass. It had fed and nourished every blossom. Had fresh new tulips sprung up overnight? Had the azaleas and rhododendrons burst into bigger and more glorious blooms? She had already been toying with the idea of taking a small group over to Peace Fields if time allowed. Now she knew she must. She would take everyone! After the initial dedication prayer, she would invite all who wanted to take the walk to go with her there. She could only imagine the magic they would experience in going, especially today. She quickly checked the computer for a weather forecast. It was going to be unseasonably warm, in the low seventies, with a slight breeze from the south.

"God, did You do this just for me!"

Normally, for an event that was to begin at two o'clock Elizabeth would have worn a robe or caftan until one, but she knew that would not work today. Adele and Kendra, and no telling how many others, would be there before eleven. Kendra and Franklin had stayed at the Curry's last night "so as not to disturb your immaculate rooms." They did want to be her very first guests, but not this time; they would have it no other way.

As she was bringing hors d'oeuvres from the freezer, Elizabeth heard Anna Louise on the porch. "I've brought fresh flowers, Ms. Elizabeth. I know you already have vases in the rooms, so I'll just get to fixing them." With that, she was gone, moving from room to room literally spreading her own ray of sunshine—in the form of yellow roses. A single rose in every bedroom and bathroom, a gigantic arrangement in the foyer and only slightly smaller ones in the parlor and dining rooms.

Just as the arrangement was being placed on the table in the foyer, the old brass doorbell jangled. Elizabeth loved the way it sounded when someone turned it hard and fast. To her it announced the arrival of a special visitor, perhaps on a special mission. As Anna Louise answered, Elizabeth entered from the dining room.

She could not imagine who would have come this early. To her relief, she found that it was a delivery boy from The Flower Shoppe. To her overwhelming surprise, she learned that he had a van load of flowers for her. Everybody from Dottie and Floyd at the diner to Janice and Hil at Cozy Corner wanted to wish her well, with flowers, no less. She, Anna Louise, and the young man began placing lovely baskets and vases anywhere and everywhere they could find a spot. She finally decided most of them could be tastefully displayed on the porches. Before even being asked, Anna Louise started taking off the cards one by one, carefully noting on the backs pertinent information about each arrangement. She placed all of them in a large file envelope, knowing Elizabeth would want to personally respond.

Soon Adele and Kendra arrived and went directly to work. Rolls were baked, cooled, and filled with chicken salad. Ham delights were warmed, cut into hors d'oeuvre-size pieces, and artfully arranged on silver trays. The punch fountain was placed on a big table just outside the kitchen door, making it convenient to fill with the jugs of chilled punch brought straight from the big refrigerator.

Other ladies from the church began dropping in with cookies, sandwiches, fruit trays, and the like. Some stayed to help while others promised to be back by two o'clock. Over and over, Adele kept saying she was putting on the pounds just by licking spoons and bowls. One would have thought they were a professional catering team as they carefully and efficiently brought the party together, laughing, sharing stories, and thoroughly enjoying themselves all the while.

Table by table, they viewed their handiwork, pronounced it excellent, and went off in different directions to freshen up. They even put the kitchen back in pristine order before sitting at a front porch table, mint juleps in hand to await the arrival of guests.

Dedication

Anna Louise had gone to the cabin to check on Joe Bob. Just as she and her brothers walked back up the path, Bill, Carol, and a guest drove up. "There's the preacher, Sister," shouted Joe Bob. "Time to get started."

"You're right, sweetie. We'll go on up to see if we can help Ms. Elizabeth with anything. Won't be long now. Doc, you're gonna help with the parking, aren't you?"

Doc nodded. Joe Bob quickly asked, "What can I do to help Ms. Liz-beth, Sister? She'll need me to do something, won't she?"

"Yes, I will need your help, Joe Bob. I am so glad you got here early. May I say how handsome you look in your pretty green shirt and khaki slacks. You sure are a sharp dresser."

"Thank you, Ms. Liz-beth," he answered and bowed slightly. "Now, what do you want me to do?"

"If you would, I would like you to stay right here at the top of the steps to greet our guests. Since you will probably know everyone, you can call them by name and make them feel really welcome. Then you can invite them to help themselves to punch or tea and hors d'oeuvres. How does that sound?"

"That sounds just fine. I can do that. And I'll do like Sister has told me. If I don't know their names I will call them 'sir' or 'ma'am' and still welcome them."

"Yes, of course, Joe Bob. You're going to do a great job with that."

He nodded, smiled at both her and Anna Louise, and took his place at the top of the steps, awaiting the arrival of the first guests.

Bill, Carol, and the distinguished gentleman had been admiring the grounds and were now coming up the steps. "Hello, Miss Carol and Pastor Bill. Welcome to Cedar Grove. I don't know you, sir, but welcome to you, too."

No maître d' could have done better. Joe Bob took this job, as was always his manner, very seriously. He invited them to have something to eat and drink, gesturing toward the tables. "Thank you, Joe Bob. We will certainly do that," said Bill as he shook his hand. "Let me introduce Miss Carol's father to you. This is Admiral Carrol Spenser Lewis. Sir, this is my dear friend, Joe Bob Jamison."

"Glad to meet you, sir. I can remember your name 'cause it is just like Miss Carol's. Look, Sister, this is Miss Carol's daddy. Our daddy is up in heaven with our mommie, isn't he, Sister? And you told me your mommie is in heaven too, didn't you, Miss Carol?"

"Yes, I did, Joe Bob," Carol answered.

Elizabeth came over to greet the trio and mention to Bill that they needed just a moment to talk. She wanted to be sure they were on the same page about where he would stand to make the formal dedication and where the guests should be.

"Here is our lovely hostess," Bill said warmly, giving her a friendly hug. "Ms. Elizabeth Barrington, Carol's father, Admiral Carrol Spenser Lewis."

"Just Spense, ma'am. It's a pleasure to meet you. I've already heard a lot about you. What you are doing here is wonderful. You've made a lot of people very happy."

"Thank you, Admiral." Elizabeth extended her hand and smiled in such a way that allowed Mr. Lewis to anticipate her next words. He beat her to the punch.

"Yes, I really am C. S. Lewis, but if you promise not to ask me what life was really like during the Roaring Twenties, I promise not to pull navy cop on you."

Laughing heartily, Elizabeth remarked, "Obviously you read my mind, but I promise. Now that we have that out of the way, please make yourself at home. I need to speak with your son-in-law for just a moment. Carol, introduce this navy cop to our friends." *What a delightful man,* Elizabeth thought. Now she knew where Carol got those piercing blue eyes. *I bet his hair was once as dark as hers, too; however, that salt and pepper sure sets a striking contrast to his bronze skin.*

"Pastor Bill," she said as she composed herself, glancing only once over her shoulder as she walked quickly toward Bill. "What are you thinking about all this? You think maybe you should stand here on the porch, maybe at the top of the steps and our guests stand or sit in the yard? Tell me your thoughts. This is a first for me, you know."

"It may be a first, Ms. Elizabeth, but no one would ever know it. You have crossed every *t* and dotted every *i*. I think your idea is right on. We could use those chairs that are already set up and then invite folk to sit or stand. Some folk are just as comfortable standing sometimes, you know. My remarks will be very brief. Afterward we will have a short prayer. I'm sure you will have some comments as well, won't you?"

"Only a word or two. I don't think I would be able to stay composed and unemotional for more than that. Then I'm going to invite those who want to walk over to Peace Fields. If they choose to go, Anna Louise will sing for us there, one stanza of 'It Is Well with My Soul.' We'll just play all that by ear. What do you think?"

"Sounds great! We will do the dedication just when the parlor clock strikes two. I want you to look how many people are already here, and we still have a half hour to go."

Elizabeth looked around. There were people everywhere: on the porches, in the yard and still more coming up the drive. She caught a glimpse of the mayor and his wife talking with Denton and Franklin, and was that Judge Thornton with them! She had earlier seen the town newspaper van drive up, so she knew somewhere in the crowd was their photographer clicking away at unsuspecting folk.

She smiled as she headed toward Mrs. Bea, who was sitting at a table in the yard, her signature parasol cocked sideways over her head and shoulder. The glistening silver hair sported a mother-of-pearl comb placed just so. *I think I need to wake up from this Great Gatsby party dream*, she thought. *But I don't want to.*

Glad that Mrs. Bea was alone, Elizabeth greeted her with a peck on the cheek and a warm handshake. They had talked at length several weeks earlier about the business arrangement concerning their properties. They had agreed that only those who were directly involved needed to know of the details. Elizabeth quickly saw that Mrs. Bea's years had given her astute wisdom and deep compassion. No wonder the people of this community loved her so. Looking intently into Elizabeth's eyes, speaking firmly, she said, "If I can ever be of any help to you, Elizabeth, you know where I am." Elizabeth thanked her and told her how much it meant to her that she had come.

"Wouldn't have missed it for the world. Always did love a good party on somebody else's dime!" She laughed heartily and waved Elizabeth away as others came up to greet her.

Almost as if by design, several people began to set up more chairs in the yard. With the pleasant breeze and the dappled sunlight filtering through the massive oak trees, they were very comfortable as they enjoyed food and drink and the company of good friends. Just as the clock started to strike two o'clock, Bill stepped to the top of the steps.

"Greetings, dear friends. On behalf of Ms. Elizabeth Barrington and the Jamison family …" *He is so good,* Elizabeth thought. *He always knows the right thing to say.* "I want to welcome you to Cedar Grove Bed and Breakfast, Leesboro's newest neighbor and business. We have gathered today to officially welcome Ms. Barrington and to dedicate this business. If you would bow your heads with me, please.

"Father, as we humbly bow our heads and hearts before You, we lift our praise to You for Your great love for us. As did Joshua in days of old, we dedicate this house, this home, this land to You. We ask Your blessing, Your leadership, Your protection on every venture here. We know that You put all the plans together. You brought it all to pass as only You can. In Numbers 23 Your Word tells us to look and see what God hath wrought. We have seen. Praised be the name of the Lord! And in Proverbs 31 we read, 'A woman that feareth the Lord, she shall be praised' and … 'Let her own works praise her in the gates.' We give Ms. Barrington and Cedar Grove to You as she has expressed that desire, and now we praise You for what You are going to do. Amen"

A resounding "amen" echoed throughout the crowd, and then silence. Not one person moved or spoke until the young pastor raised his head. Tears filled every eye. He motioned for Elizabeth and announced, "I give you Ms. Elizabeth Barrington, our hostess, our friend." Still no one moved or spoke.

Dabbing away tears, Elizabeth went to his side. In a voice barely above a whisper she said, "My dear, dear friends. How can

I really say thank you? Today is a dream come true—one that you have helped make happen. Together, we are about to begin a wonderful journey. I sincerely believe Cedar Grove of Leesboro has been in the mind of God for a very long time. He had just allowed us the opportunity to be a part of it with Him at this time. For any of you who want to, I would like to ask you to join me at a place called Peace Fields, where we will finalize today's festivities. Joe Bob will lead the way. Thank you."

Spontaneous cheering and clapping broke out as Elizabeth stepped aside and Joe Bob waved for everyone to follow him. As they fell in line Doc spoke. "It is only a short walk but a pleasant one, and ladies, don't worry, the flagstone path will keep your nice shoes from getting dirty."

Elizabeth was puzzled. There was no flagstone path, only a well-worn dirt trail. Anticipating her question, Doc came alongside and explained. "I overheard you several days ago telling Anna that you would like to take folk to visit Peace Fields, so a few of us guys did a little work on the trail. I'm glad we were able to keep it a secret from you. I was pretty sure you would not have a chance to go there with all you were trying to do. I think you will be pleased."

Doc smiled and walked away, leaving her speechless. No sooner had he gone than someone touched her arm. In a voice that would have made Scarlett swoon, C. S. Lewis drawled, "Ma'am, may I offer my arm to escort you to your destination?" She could not keep from laughing out loud as she accepted.

Trying to match his Savannah manner, she responded, "Why, dear me, Mr. Lewis, I'd be honored." She only wished she had one of Mrs. Bea's lace parasols to perfect the moment.

They chatted amicably as they made their way with the others along the newly lain path. How had she not known what the men had been up to? She made a mental note not to be that busy in the future. They had done a superb job. The stones had been placed with great care so that there was no danger of stumbling. The bushes on either side had been trimmed away, allowing ample room for couples to walk side by side along the winding path. As she knew would be the case, everyone was overwhelmed when they got to the bridge and viewed the scene just beyond the rippling stream. Again, a hush came over them as they stepped onto the plush carpet of grass in the place of sanctuary. Without a word, Anna Louise made her way to the ancient stone altar. Turning to face the expectant crowd, she raised her angelic voice in song. When she got to the chorus she lifted her hands inviting them to join her. *"It is well, it is well with my soul!"*

Joe Bob had moved up to stand beside Elizabeth. "Oh, dear boy! Wasn't that just wonderful. I can see why you would refer to this as the place where cedars sing."

"No, Ms. Liz-beth. This is not where cedars sing. This is Gramma's Peace Fields. Where cedars sing is mine and Mommie's place!"

Was she ever going to learn exactly what that was? Was it even a real place, or was it just an enigma—a place of joy and happiness in the mind of this precious boy?

CHART THE COURSE

Almost immediately after the open house, calls began to come in at Cedar Grove. With only four rooms to rent, Elizabeth could not begin to accommodate all who desired to come. It was now mid-June, and very few nights had she been alone in the house. She had already hosted several teas, showers, and birthday parties for some of the town's folk.

Having said good-bye to the delightful Fallons from Chicago, she returned to the kitchen. Not being accustomed to Southern breakfasts, they had been overwhelmed at the spread she had put before them and the other two couples. Elizabeth loved cooking for her guests, and with Anna Louise's consistent help, it was nothing but joy.

There had been no plan at all about having help from either Anna Louise or Joe Bob, but they showed up to assist the very first guests who came. Joe Bob carried in luggage and escorted guests to their rooms. He was always conscientious to ask if they needed anything more. Anna Louise helped serve and clean up. More often than not, she would have the towels and bed linens in the wash before Elizabeth had said her last good-byes. When she tried to pay them or protested at all their work, they acted as if they were almost offended. So she graciously accepted their willing gifts of help and determined to figure out some way to reciprocate.

After the three of them had put the entire house in apple-pie order, Anna Louise took Joe Bob by the hand and directed him down the path toward the cabin. No more guests were booked until Friday, four days away, so all three of them could rest for a bit. On Thursday Elizabeth would make an early run to the market and spend the afternoon in the kitchen. After that, she would have a couple of days to take a breather and catch up on some paperwork. The next big event for Cedar Grove was the bridal shower for one of the young women from the church. That would require a lot of cooking and preparation, so a little lull was welcomed.

After service on Wednesday night, Adele came running up to Elizabeth. "I need to talk to you for just a minute," she said breathlessly.

"Sure. Is everything okay?" Elizabeth asked.

"Yes, yes. Everything's fine. Just need a favor if you can."

"You know I'll try, Adele. What is it?"

"I need a room for a week or ten days if you have one, starting Sunday night," Adele said expectantly.

Elizabeth was flabbergasted. "What? Why do you need a room?" she spluttered.

"Oh, good grief, girl; it's not for me!" Adele doubled over laughing. "Did ya think Denton was kicking me out?"

"I didn't know what to think!" Elizabeth sighed with relief. "Now, go back to the beginning. When again do you need the room? And who is it for?"

Adele was still laughing. "Let's sit here for a minute. That was just too funny! Took all the breath out of me. Here's the deal," Adele said as they made themselves comfortable on the steps.

"Denton has been thinking of bringing a new person into the firm. He interviewed dozens of applicants and prayed over each one. He has finally made a decision, and now the new man will be here on Sunday evening, but his place isn't ready yet. He's a single young man, and he's taking that new, little apartment over The Flower Shoppe. It's going to be ideal for him, but they don't have all the painting done yet or the carpet down. They assured me it will only be a few days more. I'd keep him myself but my sister—you remember Mitzi. Well, she and her little grandson, Evan, are coming on Saturday, and Lord only knows how long they will stay this time. Evan's conduct kinda determines that. I always love having them, but sometimes it's just not convenient, don't you know." Adele was talking hard and fast, as if she must get it all said and get an answer before the clock struck again.

"Slow down, girl," Elizabeth said, standing and taking Adele by the shoulders. "Slow down before you have a stroke."

They both laughed uproariously. "I do get carried away, don't I? No one can ever say I don't have passion!"

"That's for sure," Elizabeth joked good-naturedly. "I'll have to make sure I can move a guest to another room, but I'll make it work. Let me check everything out when I get home. I'll call you first thing in the morning."

"I knew you'd come to my rescue. What did I ever do before God brought you to me?" She hugged Elizabeth hard and bade her good-bye. "Better get home and make sure Denton *hasn't* kicked me out." She laughed and sprinted to her car as fast as her stilettos would allow. Elizabeth stood watching, a big grin on her face. Only for church did Adele wear heels and feminine, flowing skirts. Normally, she would have on slacks and sensible shoes or maybe even jeans and sneakers. She was quite a character, but she got the job done. She was the first friend Elizabeth had made in Leesboro, and that friendship was growing deeper by the day.

As Elizabeth looked over the reservation sheets, she realized the only room she could make work for several days for the young lawyer was the big one with the three twin beds. She leaned back in her chair, clasped her hands behind her head, and smiled. Again, God's timing and His provision amazed her. She had almost left behind the big mattress topper, but at the last minute, for some reason, she had put it on the truck. It had been stored in the attic, still in its carrying case for the whole time she had been here. Actually, she had almost forgotten about it. Now, it was time to bring it down, unroll it on the tables in the backyard, and allow the sun and air to re-freshen it and make it usable. As had been its original design, it would be placed atop two side-by-side twin beds, converting them into a king. In doing that, the large room would be exactly what Mr. Patrick Bryant, attorney-at-law, would need.

Adele hadn't said anything about what personal items he would be bringing, but knowing Adele, she was sure she had a workable plan for whatever. Elizabeth would address that as well as his meals, etc., when she called Adele in the morning. The next few days were now going to be busier than she had planned, but she knew what was happening was a good thing. As so many times before, Elizabeth had no way of knowing what God's next designed plan was.

In short order Elizabeth had ironed out all the details with Adele and gotten the room ready for young Patrick. She was glad the king bedspread from her room would match the color scheme in his. She would be fine with the antique white coverlet for her bed; well-worn though it was, it held many fond memories. With two of the twin beds pushed together in the middle of the room and one taken out, it had a feeling of spaciousness. She had moved furniture from room to room in the very beginning with no real rhyme or reason, just until her eye was pleased with each arrangement.

Looking now at this room, she marveled. The massive dresser and chest of drawers certainly suited the king bed. The old desk in front of the window facing west allowed a wonderful place to sit and work and watch the glorious sunset. *After he's gone,* Elizabeth thought, *I may very well come here as a daily ritual. The distant mountains, the setting sun, and the faraway, lonesome sound of the afternoon train whistle could carry one's thoughts to another time and place. Yes, this room is good; a great place to rest and think and shed the burdens of the day. I don't know, but I have a feeling any person who deals with today's justice system on a regular basis would need such a place.*

On Friday, two couples came in: Mr. and Mrs. Lynn and Mr. and Mrs. Brewer. Strange as it might be, the Lynns were retired missionaries, having served in China for more than forty years. The Brewers were now preparing to go to the Philippines. Meeting at Cedar Grove for the first time, they instantly found that they had much to talk about. Their fields of service, their ages, and their ministry gifts were very different, but as they talked they, as well as Elizabeth, couldn't help but feel that they had been providentially brought together. Both couples were happy to attend services with Elizabeth on Sunday morning. She couldn't help but think that God was allowing her to have a part in the lives of some of His special servants. She prayed that He would continue to use her. Was this one of the reasons He had given her thoughts of a bed and breakfast in the first place?

She had heard it said many times that God would put a person into His service using the gifts, talents, and loves that He had already given them. To that, He would add the abilities needed once a person was willing to be used. Why, she had even told people that herself. She believed that, knew it to be true. Was it time for her to look into a mirror somewhere? Elizabeth's home and her business had been dedicated to God from the very beginning. It was overwhelmingly exciting to rest in Him in anticipation of what would be next on the horizon.

As Elizabeth was leaving the church parking lot, Adele yelled to tell her she would call as soon as Patrick showed up. Her guests had gone their separate ways for the afternoon, so she ate a quick lunch and tidied their rooms. She refused to allow Anna Louise to help on Sundays. Many of the guests checked out on Sunday, so she often left the rooms until the next day. When they did stay over, she did minimal maid service by herself. She still had not gotten comfortable with Anna Louise doing so much, anyway.

By the time Adele called, Elizabeth had finished all the little necessary chores and had even had a chance to rest a bit. Sunday was God's day, and she had always made it a point to do no more work than was absolutely necessary. Attending church services and spending extra time in the Word and in prayer were very important to her. When she didn't have guests, she would often take the time to visit on Sunday afternoons. There was always someone from the church or community in the hospital or on the sick list. Pastor Bill and Carol didn't want to burden her, but they so appreciated her helping with the visiting. Bill jokingly told her that he thought people enjoyed her visits more than his.

"They just consider it my job," he would say. "They know when you come it's because you want to—a visit from a friend who cares!"

Adele was telling her that Patrick would get to her house just in time to join them for evening services, so if it were okay with Elizabeth, they would come to Cedar Grove afterward. "And," Adele went on, "he's only bringing his clothes and personal items as if it were any road trip. He'll go back for the rest once he sees what the apartment will accommodate. Isn't that a smart idea? I think I'm gonna like this kid."

"Yes. Me too, Adele. That all sounds just fine. He can just follow me back after service, and you won't even need to come down—I mean unless you want to. Oh, you know what I mean," sputtered Elizabeth.

Adele laughed. "Of course I know what you mean, and that will be perfect." She chatted on about nothing for a few minutes and then bid her friend good-bye. How wonderful it was to have such a dear friend who understood her heart.

Patrick settled in, assuring Elizabeth he would be quite comfortable. He even made mention of the desk and the view from his window. He came down early each morning and took a long walk before leaving for the day. He accepted only cereal, fruit, juice, and coffee for breakfast promising to linger and enjoy a big meal with her and the other guests on a day when he wasn't headed to the office.

Little Boy Lost

On Wednesday Elizabeth decided to have a little impromptu lunch for Adele and Mitzi since she would be leaving on Saturday. She asked Bill and Carol to join them. Anna Louise and Joe Bob had already agreed to help her, and since Doc came home for lunch when he could, he would try to join them. It was a joy for Elizabeth to extend hospitality to this little circle of friends who had become like family to her.

Joe Bob and Evan had gone outside to "work off some of that energy," as Mitzi said. They could be heard yelling and shrieking as little boys do. Suddenly the sounds were different. They had gone from sounds of play to those of pain and terror. Joe Bob came running and screaming into the dining room.

"Come, come quick! Evan ... fell ... hurt! Come!" Chairs were shoved from their places as every person in the room responded.

"I didn't do it, Sister! I didn't hurt him!" Joe Bob screamed hysterically.

"Of course you didn't, honey. Just tell us what happened," said Anna Louise as she tried to calm her totally distraught brother. She caught him and held him close, crooning to him, gently rocking him back and forth.

By now the others had reached the injured child, writhing on the ground in pain. His sobs had lessened in volume; he was now moaning and groaning. When Doc reached him, he feared he was going into shock. His skin was clammy, his eyes rolling back. Taking charge, he began calmly talking to Evan, telling him everything was going to be all right, while at the same time sending Elizabeth back into the house for a blanket.

"I need to check your arm, son, so try to be as still as you can. Then we'll get you to the hospital to get you fixed up." His gentle manner seemed to calm the frightened boy. He covered him with the blanket after quickly assessing the damage to the arm. Adele was doing her best to keep Mitzi from going off the deep end.

"Doc will do whatever needs to be done, little sister. He'll know just what to do."

By this time, the others were piecing together the story of the accident. Evan and Joe Bob had been playing with a Frisbee. It had sailed over Evan's head and landed on top of the big boulder at the edge of the yard. Evan started to try to climb up for it with Joe Bob begging him not to. Just as he started to grasp it, his foot slipped, and he tumbled down the side of the rock. He must have tried to catch himself with his right hand, but instead he landed squarely on it.

"Bill," said Doc authoritatively, "Call the ER. Tell them I'm bringing Evan in for some x-rays. I don't think his arm is broken, but I can't be absolutely sure without some pictures. I don't want to do anything right now, but we do want to hurry before any more swelling occurs. Mrs. Randolph, let's take him in Adele's car. That way you can sit in the backseat with him. He needs to be as still as possible. I think he is just fine except for that arm—no other bumps, bruises, or anything actually. Right now he is just very scared."

Doc carefully picked Evan up and placed him in the back seat of Adele's waiting car. With his head in Mitzi's lap, he could comfortably ride the short distance to the medical center. Without hesitation, he jumped behind the wheel and was speeding away even before Adele got her door shut.

"We'll be praying, Mitzi," Elizabeth called after them.

"And I will follow in my car," said Pastor Bill as he sprinted away.

Doc calmly explained to Mitzi and Adele what would happen at the hospital. He told them he thought the elbow was dislocated and that the arm was not broken. Of course, there was no way to really know without the x-rays. If that were the problem, it could be maneuvered back into place with minimal pain and would be as good as new immediately.

As the technician took Evan to the lab, Doc began to explain more fully what would be done. "More than likely," he went on, "they will somewhat numb the area with ice, inject a local anesthetic into the joint, and quickly put it back into place. With some distracting from you, he may not even realize what has happened."

By now Bill had joined the group and was trying to help reassure Mitzi. He, too, knew that Doc's diagnoses were most often right on target. "Let's wait just a few minutes before you call your daughter. Don't want to unnecessarily alarm her."

Shortly the ER doctor entered with a smile and a good word. "Ma'am," he addressed an anxious Mitzi. "Your grandson is fine. No broken bones, just a dislocated elbow. If you'll come with me, I'll explain what we need to do."

Mitzi glanced back at Doc and with a sigh of relief, followed the doctor. He began telling her almost verbatim what Doc had said. "And if you'll just sit next to him, perhaps hold his hand

and engage him in some distracting conversation, we'll have him fixed up in no time."

Doc excused himself, telling the waiting group he would be right back. Each one of them had entered a personal, private arena of prayer so paid little attention to his pensiveness. He walked slowly around the grounds just outside the ER, his mind muddled with a myriad of thoughts. He hadn't realized how distracted he had been from the present or how long he had been there until Bill was patting his shoulder and calling his name.

"Oh, sorry, Pastor. I didn't know you were here. Is everything okay?"

"Yes, yes. The boy is fine ... and so are Grandma and Auntie. I think they were in as much pain as he, but everything is fine. They're just picking out a cool sling for him and finalizing his checkout. Mrs. Randolph has already called her daughter, who didn't seem to be nearly as concerned as all of us were. She said he was forever getting into all kinds of scrapes, and she was sure we had handled it fine. I'm going to call Carol now to let her know we are on our way back. You ready to go?"

"Yeah, yeah. I'm good. Boy, I'm glad that kid is okay. It could have been much worse. You know, I did that very same thing when I was just about his age; fell off that same ol' rock. Boys just think they're invincible, don't they?"

"Yes, *they* sure do." Bill laughed as they walked back to collect the ladies and Evan. "Good thing we grow up and get past that idea, isn't it?"

As they entered the waiting area, Adele was thanking the doctor and chatting with the staff people. Evan, sporting a sling with a Colts logo, was obviously none the worse for wear. He had been a brave patient who was now being rewarded with lollipops and stickers.

"I still haven't called Carol yet," Bill remarked just as his phone rang. "And there she is now ... going to fuss at me for not letting them know."

"Hey, hon," he said pleasantly into the phone. "I was just ..." She cut him off. His smile faded, his brow furrowed. "What? What do you mean, you can't find him?" He looked at Doc and the others, holding up his hand signaling for them to hold on.

Something was very wrong. He was listening intently. "Okay, Carol. We're on our way. Be there in just a few minutes. Listen, tell them we will find him ... not to worry."

"What's going on, Bill?" Adele asked first. "Find who?"

"Carol says Joe Bob is missing. They've looked everywhere for him. Anna knew he was upset about Evan, but she thought he had just gone to his room the way he does when he's upset or doesn't understand something. After they finished cleaning up, she went to see about him, but he wasn't there. They searched the houses, barns, sheds ... everywhere, even went to Peace Fields. He seems to have vanished. He just isn't there!"

"Get in," Doc ordered as he jumped behind the wheel of Adele's Jeep. "Let's go!"

"I'm calling Denton, Doc. He can come help us look," Adele said as she closed the door behind Mitzi and Evan and jumped in beside Doc. He raced out of the lot, almost jerking the door out of her hand.

Evan had remained quiet but now spoke. "Joe Bob kept telling me he was sorry, like he thought he had hurt me, but he didn't! It wasn't his fault; I just fell. Please find him. I gotta make him understand that he is my friend and he didn't do anything to hurt me." He buried his face against his grandmother and sobbed. Now he felt responsible for his friend running away.

Anna Louise, tears streaming down her face, ran to Doc. "What are we going to do, Doc? We have looked everywhere!"

"I know, honey. I know. Now just calm down, and let's decide what we need to do. We've all been asking God to show us what we need to do, and I'm sure He will."

Before he had finished speaking, Denton Curry came racing up the drive. He had barely come to a stop before Patrick Bryant leapt from the passenger seat. Without any hesitation Patrick was at Anna Louise's side, gathering her into his arms. She collapsed into him, allowing him to hold her trembling body. After several moments they seemed to realize their actions and embarrassedly stepped away from each other.

"I ... I'm sorry," Patrick stammered

"It's okay, Patrick. You were only being kind, trying to comfort. Thank you."

Anna Louise's voice was almost a whisper as she slowly moved away from him. Obviously shaken, she hoped those standing around would not be able to see what was going on with her. Even she didn't understand the fluttering of her heart.

Quickly, the men devised a plan as to who would go where. Doc and Bill would go one way, Denton and Patrick another. It was only early afternoon, and they felt sure they could find Joe Bob before any worry of darkness. The ladies and Evan slowly entered the parlor, joined hands, and entered into a time of intercessory prayer. Just as they were ending the prayer, Elizabeth almost screamed at Anna Louise.

"Anna, I think I may know where he has gone! Quick, let's you and I change into jeans and boots."

Bewildered, Anna Louise complied without hesitation. As Elizabeth ran to her room to change, Anna Louise went racing to the cabin to do the same. There was no time for explanation as Elizabeth emerged ready for hiking. She told the others to continue in prayer as she confidently added, "I really believe we will find him and return soon."

No sooner had she left the back steps than she was joined by Anna Louise. She didn't know from where her confidence had come except from a loving, caring God. She quickly questioned a waiting Anna Louise. "Anna, do you know anything about this place that Joe Bob refers to as *where cedars sing*," or is that just an imaginary place with him?"

Anna Louise was stunned. She stammered, "Yes, yes. I know ... I think I know ... what he means. There was a place where Mama took us when we were kids, a place she referred to that way. But I haven't been there in years. I'm not even sure I can still find it. Joe Bob loved that place. You think he may have gone there? Why? How?"

"I don't know, dear girl. I don't have any real answers, but for some reason I think we should try to look there. Do you even know which way to start?"

"I ... I do remember we would go down a trail from behind the old, big barn ... the one we never use anymore. It was quite a long walk, but as children we were running and playing as we went, trusting Mama to take us. You know how kids are, just blindly skipping along, chasing butterflies, running from bees, picking flowers. Oh, it was such a long, long time ago, Ms. Elizabeth; I just don't know!"

"Of course, honey. I do understand; but we'll try," Elizabeth reassured her as they hurried down the path toward the barn. Elizabeth was reprimanding herself for not having looked over all the land before now, but how was she to know how important it would be? The diligent work of Doc and Joe Bob as well as the grazing of the farm animals had kept the weeds under control in this area. However, what they would encounter up ahead was anybody's guess.

"I can't believe this, Ms. Elizabeth," Anna Louise quietly said. "The trail feels so familiar, as if I traveled it only yesterday. And look, it isn't even overgrown. Isn't that just too strange?"

"I know, but you are absolutely right. I expected we would be forced to claw our way through bushes and briars and no telling what, but this is unbelievable. We seem to be on a much-traveled hiking trail, and the scenery is breathtaking."

What Elizabeth didn't share with Anna Louise were the ominous questions that kept racing through her mind. What *would* they encounter just around the next curve or over the next rise? Had some unscrupulous characters been using this hidden place for some criminal activities? Or were they going to run head-long into some *"hippie"* group? *Oh, my,* she thought. *What are we walking into?* Yet, she felt compelled to continue.

Both women were growing weary, hot, and more concerned, yet they pushed on. The trail had become more narrow, but as they rounded another little curve, they entered a clearing. At first when Anna Louise stopped, Elizabeth feared something was dreadfully wrong. She gasped and with eyes wild with excitement screamed, "Oh, Ms. Elizabeth! This is it! We're almost there!"

She began to run on legs that had gained new strength. Elizabeth was doing her best to keep up. Across the clearing they raced, into a thick stand of trees. Elizabeth heard the sound of a stream just ahead, and as the late afternoon winds came down the hollow, she thought she heard music. Anna Louise stopped just short of exiting the grove, turned to look at Elizabeth through tear-filled eyes, and whispered, "This is the place where cedars sing! Can you hear them? Listen!"

Never had Elizabeth been so spellbound! Stepping out of the trees, she saw a magical, glistening waterfall that seemed to be tumbling out of the very sky. An enormous stand of ancient, majestic cedar trees were standing as sentinels on either side.

There near the pool of sparkling water sat Joe Bob, swaying back and forth to the rhythm of the wind and water. This *was* music! Music of nature! A song for any listening ear! Surely a balm for any hurting spirit! Did David play harp melodies for Saul any more lovely than this? Never had the songs of birds been so beautiful. This special thick stand of cedars must have been home to scores of song birds. They must have been placed in this special place for a most important task. The soothing melodies of nature, from stirring winds and swaying trees to thundering waters, filled this paradise. Overcome with the serenity and the beauty of their surroundings and the relief of finding their precious boy, both women, sister and friend, worshiped without a word.

Slowly Joe Bob turned, smiled, and rose to meet them as if this were a normal daily activity. "Sister! Ms. Liz-beth! You came to where cedars sing." He hugged them both. "I'm sure glad you have come to mine and Mommie's place. You've been wanting to come, haven't you, Ms. Liz-beth? Now you can come all by yourself if you want … but I might like to come with you some of the times. I've been talking to Mommie. I told her you would come someday, and she was real glad. Ready to go back home now?"

With that, he grasped Elizabeth with one hand and Anna Louise with the other and started toward the trail through the trees. He had no idea that he had been the object of a frantic search, that those who cared for him so deeply had been consumed with worry and fear.

"Is little Evan okay, Sister? I didn't mean for him to be hurt. Is he mad at me? I told Mommie all about what happened, and she said he would be okay. And Mommie is always right, isn't she, Sister?"

"Yes, honey. Mommie is always right. Little Evan is just fine; he's waiting for you back at the house. He knows you didn't want him to get hurt, and he's not at all mad at you. He says you are his very special friend."

"I am. I am his special friend. I'm gonna go give him a hug!" Before anything more could be said, he had broken free from them and was running toward home as fast as his little legs would allow.

They would ask him for verification later, but both women knew that he was the one who had kept the path clean and clear for what must have been many, many lone trips to *where cedars sing!* One of the most basic needs of all humankind is to have a place of sanctuary. Had God used the strange events of this day to show Elizabeth where that place was for her? Did He allow one of His children to feel pain and others fear and sadness in order for her to be brought to her special place?

Epilogue

Would Elizabeth Barrington, innkeeper at Cedar Grove, find much more than she was looking for in Leesboro, Virginia? She had come here—had been divinely led here—to have a sense of place; a place where she could work and worship and move on with her life. She had not burned bridges, for she knew there was the great possibility that she at some time would be drawn back to her past. The past is never completely gone—it is always there, reminding one of mistakes made, lessons learned, roads less traveled. However, the future was before her, and she would embrace it the very best she could, trembling sometimes, nevertheless with assurance that there would be continuing blessings and places for service. She had recently read something about the people that are placed in our lives—some for a reason, some for a season, and some for a lifetime. It was going to be interesting and even intriguing to see in which category all these new friends belonged!

    She smiled as she began to think of her many new friends. How people like Adele Curry, Miss Bea, Carol and Bill, and even Spence Lewis were going to impact her life she could not begin to imagine. She knew that some of them had begun to wonder about her secrets and her days of melancholia, but she was not yet ready to revisit that pain. Would she ever be? What she did not know—could not know—was that these beautiful people were going to travel with her into her past and bring her into a future filled with beauty and promise beyond her wildest dreams.

None of them knew anything about her family; none of them had asked about her past, where she really came from, and why she had chosen their sleepy little village. She knew the day would come when she would need to reveal some of those things ... but not today! Today was hers to enjoy without looking backward ... or even forward. Today was hers to just be here ... to be here right now without any ties, without any bonds, without any pain! She must hold it as tightly as she could ... for this moment. She knew that it could soon be gone.

Even as Elizabeth reveled in this great, overwhelming joy, there was a giant plane on a runway at Heathrow preparing to lift off. The beautiful young woman in 23C appeared poised and confident—at least as much as any British girl of fifteen could. Her traveling companions had assured her that all would be well, but she was not so sure. Her whole world had changed in a moment, and now it would be taking on another totally different dimension—as would that of the lady on the other side of the pond.

About the Author

Elizabeth Sue Hyde, native of Bryson City, North Carolina, is a resident of Marion, North Carolina. She is the author of three other books: *Blue Willow Dishes, Gone Full Circle,* and her latest, *From the Kitchen, From the Heart.*

She is a mother of three, grandmother of seven (and one "grafted in" grandson, Brittany's husband, Kyle.)

Sue loves traveling and acting, is an avid reader, and has always been passionate about storytelling and writing. Nothing brings her more joy than sharing stories about her family, as she has done with her other books.

Where Cedars Sing is her first novel and is in no way like her preceding books. She feels that it has a higher purpose. She plans to fund a relief effort for the earthquake victims in Nepal from the proceeds of its sales.

"This manuscript had been on the computer for several years. The week before the April 25, 2015, earthquake in Nepal, I was drawn to it. A series of events then led me to know that it was time to publish. The story is one of recovery, triumph over adversity, and stepping out in faith."

Jeremiah 29:11

Printed in the United States
By Bookmasters